Opening my eyes I saw my own body, a sack
of diseases and old flesh, very nearly dead.
That body stirred; its eyes opened—to darkness; its hands moved up to its face; its face
screamed . . .

CAMP CONCENTRATION

"A commanding book—both daring and suc-
cessfully so."

—Brian W. Aldiss

CAMP CONCENTRATION

Thomas M. Disch

CAMP CONCENTRATION

*A Bantam Book / published by arrangement with
the author*

Bantam edition / February 1980

ISBN 0–553–13117–6

Published simultaneously in the United States and Canada

---

*Bantam Books are published by Bantam Books, Inc. Its trade-
mark, consisting of the words "Bantam Books" and the por-
trayal of a bantam, is Registered in U.S. Patent and Trademark
Office and in other countries. Marca Registrada. Bantam
Books, Inc., 666 Fifth Avenue, New York, New York 10019.*

This book is dedicated,
with thanks,
to John Sladek and
Thomas Mann,
two good writers.

Now, reader, I have told my dream to thee;
See if thou canst interpret it to me,
Or to thyself, or neighbor. But take heed
Of misinterpreting; for that, instead
Of doing good, will but thyself abuse.
By misinterpreting evil issues.

Take heed, also, that thou be not extreme,
In playing with the outside of my dream.
Nor let my figure, or similitude,
Put thee into a laughter or a feud;
Leave this for boys and fools; but as for thee,
Do thou the substance of my matter see.

Put by the curtains; look within my veil;
Turn up my metaphors and do not fail.
There, if thou seekst them, such things to find,
As will be helpful to an honest mind.

What of my dross thou findest there, be bold
To throw away, but yet preserve the gold.
What if my gold be wrapped in ore?
None throws away the apple for the core.
But if thou shalt cast all away as vain,
I know not but 'twill make me dream again.

John Bunyan,
The Pilgrim's Progress

BOOK ONE

May 11

Young R.M., my Mormon guard, has brought me a
supply of paper at last. It is three months to the day since
I first asked him for some. Inexplicable, this change of
heart. Perhaps Andrea has been able to get a bribe to
him. Rigor Mortis denies it, but then he would deny it.
We talked politics, and I was able to gather from hints
R.M. let drop that President McNamara has decided to
use "tactical" nuclear weapons. Perhaps, therefore, it is to
McNamara, not to Andrea, that I am indebted for this
paper, since R.M. has been fretting these many weeks that
General Sherman, poor General Sherman, has been denied
adequate hitting power. When, as today, R.M. is happy,
his fearful smile, those thin lips pulled back tightly across
the perfect deathshead teeth, flickers into being at the
slightest pretense of humor. Why do all the Mormons I
have known have that same constipated smile? Is their
toilet training exceptionally severe?

This is my journal. I can be candid here. Candidly, I
could not be more miserable.

May 12

Journals, such as I have erewhile attempted, have a
way of becoming merely exhortatory. I must remember,
here, to be circumstantial from the start, taking as model
that sublime record of prison existence, *The House of the
Dead*. It should be easy to be circumstantial here: not
since childhood has mere circumstance so tyrannized me.
The two hours each day before dinner are spent in a
Gethsemane of dread and hope. Dread lest we be served
that vile spaghetti once again. Hope that there may be a

3

good hunk of meat in my ladle of stew, or an apple for dessert. Worse than "chow" is each morning's mad spate of scrubbing and polishing to prepare our cells for inspection. The cells are as bony-clean as a dream of Philip Johnson (Grand Central Bathroom), while we, the prisoners, carry about with us the incredible, ineradicable smell of our stale, wasted flesh.

However, we lead here no worse a life than we would be leading now outside these walls had we answered our draft calls. Nasty as this prison is, there is this advantage to it—that it will not lead so promptly, so probably, to death. Not to mention the inestimable advantage of righteousness.

Ah, but who is this "we"? Besides myself there are not more than a dozen other conchies here, and we are kept carefully apart, to prevent the possibility of esprit. The prisoners—the *real* prisoners—hold us in contempt. They have that more sustaining advantage than righteousness—guilt. So our isolation, *my* isolation, becomes ever more absolute. And, I fear, my self-pity. There are evenings when I sit here *hoping* that R.M. will come by to argue with me.

Four months! And my sentence is for five years. . . . That is the Gorgon of all my thoughts.

May 13

I must speak of Smede. Warden Smede, my arch enemy. Smede the arbitrary, who still refuses me library privileges, allows me only a New Testament and a prayer book. It is as though I had been left, as was so often threatened, for my summer vacation with the loathed Uncle Morris of my childhood (who counseled my parents that I would "lose my eyes" by reading too much). Bald, booming, fat with the fatness of a ruined athlete: Smede. One might despise him only for having such a name. Today I learned from the small portion of my monthly letter from Andrea that the censor (Smede?) had not blacked out that the proofs of *The Hills of Switzerland*, which had been sent to me here, were returned to the publisher with a note explaining the rules for correspondents with prisoners. That was three months ago. The book is in print now. It has been *reviewed!* (I suspect the publisher hurried so in the hope of getting a little free publicity from the trial.)

The censor, naturally, removed the review Andrea had enclosed. Agonies of vanity. For ten years I could lay claim to no book but my wretched doctor's thesis on Winstanley; now my poems are in print—and it may be another five years before I'm allowed to see them. May Smede's eyes rot like potatoes in spring! May he convulse with the Malaysian palsies!

Have tried to go on with the cycle of "Ceremonies." Can't. The wells are dry, dry.

May 14

Spaghetti.

On nights like this (I write these notes after lights-out, by the glow of the perpetual twenty-watter above the toilet bowl) I wonder if I have done the right thing in electing to come here, if I'm not being a fool. Is this the stuff of heroism? or of masochism? In private life my conscience was never so conscientious. But, damn it, this war is *wrong!*

I had thought (I had convinced myself) that coming here voluntarily would be little different from joining a Trappist monastery, that my deprivations would easily be bearable if freely chosen. One of my regrets as a married man has always been that the contemplative life, in its more rarefied aspects, has been denied me. I fancied asceticism some rare luxury, a spiritual truffle. Ha!

On the bunk beneath mine a Mafia petit bourgeois (snared on tax evasion charges) snores his content. Bedsprings squeak in the visible darkness. I try to think of Andrea. In high school Brother Wilfred counseled that when lustful thoughts arose we should pray to the Blessed Virgin. Perhaps it worked for him.

May 15

Nel mezzo del camin di nostra vita indeed! My thirty-fifth birthday, and a slight case of the horrors. For a few moments this morning, before the metal shaving mirror, my double, Louie II, was in the ascendant. He mocked and raged and muddied the banner of faith, not to mention hope (already quite muddy these days), with his scurrilities. I remembered the dismal summer of my fifteenth year, the summer that Louie II was in sole possession of my soul. Dismal? Actually, there was a good deal of exhilaration in saying *Non serviam,* an exhilaration that is still confused with my first memories of sex.

Is my present situation so very much different? Except that now, prudently, I say *Non serviam* to Caesar rather than to God.

When the chaplain came by to hear my confession I didn't speak of these scruples. In his innocence he would have been apt to take the side of the cynical Louie II. But he has learned by now not to employ the meager resources of his casuistry against me (another retrograde Irish Thomist, he) and pretends to accept me at my own moral valuation. "But beware, Louis," he counseled, before absolving me, "beware of intellectual pride." Meaning, I have always supposed, beware of intellect.

How to distinguish between righteousness and self-will? Between the two Louies? How, once committed, to stop *questioning?* (That is the question. Does someone like R.M. have such problems? He gives the impression of never having had a doubt in his whole life—and Mormons seem to have so much more to doubt.

I am being less than charitable. Those wells, too, are drying up.

May 16

We were sent out of the prison today on a detail to cut down and burn blighted trees. A new virus, or one of our own, gone astray. The landscape outside the prison is, despite the season, nearly as desolate as that within. The war has at last devoured the reserves of our affluence and is damaging the fibers of the everyday.

Returning, we had to file through the clinic to get our latest inoculations. The doctor in charge held me back after the others had left. A moment's panic: Had he recognized in me the symptoms of one of the war's new diseases? No, it was to show me the review of *The Hills of S!* Bless, bless. Mons in *New Dissent*. She liked it (hurray) though she took exception, expectably, to the fetish poems. She also missed the references to Rilke, which I so labored over. Weh! While I read the review the good doctor injected what seemed like several thousand cc's of bilgy ook into my thigh; in my happiness I scarcely noticed. A review—I am *real!* Must write a letter to Mons, thanking her. Perhaps R.M. will mail it for me. Maybe I'll even be able to start writing again.

May 17

The two faggots with whom, grudgingly, the Mafia and I share our cell (it is not, you will observe, *theirs*) are suddenly not speaking to each other. Donny sits on the can all day and tinkles blues. Peter broods butchly on his bunk. Occasionally Donny will address a loud complaint to me, concerning Peter's promiscuities, real or imagined.

(When do they find opportunities for unfaithfulness?)
Donny, younger and black, is feminine, even in his bitchi-
ness, which is skilled and futile. Peter, at thirty, is still
rather handsome, though his face has a seamy, second-
hand look. They are both here on narcotics charges,
though it is Peter's distinction that he once stood trial for
murder. One gets the impression that he regrets having
been acquitted. Their passion has too much of the element
of necessity about it to be quite convincing: If you were
the only boy in the world, and I were the only other. Now
who's being bitchy?

I must say, though, that I find this sort of thing more
palatable at second hand—in Genet, for instance. My
liberality balks before the real thing.

So there is, in this context, an advantage in being as fat
as I am. No one in his right mind would lust after *this*
body.

I had thought once of doing an inspirational book for
fat people called *Fifteen Famous Fatsos*. Dr. Johnson,
Alfred Hitchcock, Salinger, Thomas Aquinas, Melchior,
Buddha, Norbert Wiener, etc.

The bedsprings are quiet tonight, but ever and again,
between the Mafia's snores, Donny or Peter heaves a sigh.

May 18

An hour this evening with young Rigor Mortis. The
epithet may be unjust, since R.M. is the nearest thing to a
friend that I've found here. He is, for all his orthodoxies,
serious-minded, a man of goodwill, and our talks are, I
hope, more than exercises in rhetoric. For my own part, I
know that I feel, beyond my evangelistic urge to bring
him round, an almost desperate desire to understand him,
for it is R.M. and his like who perpetuate this incredible
war, who believe, with a sincerity I cannot call into doubt,
that in doing so they perform a moral action. Or am I to
accept the thesis of our neo-Millsians (neo-Machiavellians,

rather), who maintain that the electorate is simply practiced upon, the groundlings of this world drama, that their secret masters in the Olympus of Washington mold their opinions as easily as they (admittedly) control the press.

I might even wish that were so. If persuasion were so easy a task, perhaps the few voices of righteousness might hope to have some effect. But it is a fact that not I nor anyone I've known on the Committee for a Unilateral Peace has ever convinced anyone of the folly and immorality of this war who was not at heart already of like mind, who needed no convincing but only our reassurances.

Perhaps Andrea is right; perhaps I should leave the war to the politicians and the propagandists—the experts, as they are called. (Just so, Eichmann was noted as an "expert" on the Jewish problem. After all, he spoke Yidish!) Abandon controversy that I may consecrate my talents exclusively to the Muses.

And my soul, then, to the Devil?

No, though opposition is a hopeless task, acquiescence would be worse. Consider Youngerman's case: *He* acquiesced, he left well enough alone, he muzzled conscience. Did irony sustain him? Or the Muses? When you rise to deliver a commencement address and half the audience walks out, where is your lofty indifference then, O poet? And his last book—so bad, so bad!

But Youngerman at least knew the meaning of his silence. When I speak to R.M. the language itself seems to alter. I grasp at meanings and they flit away, like minnows in a mountain stream. Or, a better metaphor, it is like one of those secret doors that one used to see in horror movies. It appears to be part of the bookcase, but when the hidden spring is released it turns around and its reverse side is a rough stone face. Must try and develop that image.

The last word on R.M.: We do not, and I fear we cannot, understand each other. I sometimes wonder if the reason isn't simply that he's very stupid.

May 19

The Muse descends—characteristically assuming the mortal guise of an attack of diarrhea, abetted by headache. Auden observes somewhere (in the "Letter to Lord Byron"?) how often a poet's finer flights are due/rumpty-tumpty-tumpty to the flu.

Though a small paradox, it should go without saying that I have not felt so well in months. In honor of the occasion, I will transcribe my little poem (the slightest of lyrics, but Lord! how long it has been since the last one):

The Silkworm Song

How can I possibly   Be ready to enter
That cedarwood box   Isn't it obvious
          It isn't time
          I'm in my prime

The dew is scarcely dry   Behind my ears
Words cannot describe   My tears
          And the singing
          Listen to it
The very stones are dumb   With ecstasy
How can I possibly   Go down

In that darkness   Leaving my soul behind
Listen to the singing   Butterflies
          And broken pots
          Come into the box
No no I may not   Stop the spinning
Of butterflies and broken pots   O stop

[Here the handwritten portion of Louis Sacchetti's journal ends. All the following passages were typed on a different size and stock of paper. Ed.]

10

June 2

I am being held prisoner! I have been kidnapped from the prison where I by law belong and brought to a prison in which I do not belong. Legal advice is denied me. My protests are ignored with maddening blandness. Not since the playground tyrannies of childhood have the rules of the game been so utterly and arrogantly abrogated, and I am helpless to cope. To whom shall I complain? There is not even a chaplain in this place, I'm told. Only God hears me now, and my guards.

In Springfield I was a prisoner for a stated reason, for a fixed term. Here (wherever that may be) nothing is stated, there are no rules. I demand incessantly to be returned to Springfield, but the only answer I receive is to have waved in my face the slip of paper that Smede signed approving my transfer. Smede would have approved my being gassed, if it came to that. Damn Smede! Damn these new anonymities in their spiff, black, un-identifying uniforms! Damn me, for having been fool enough to place myself in a situation where this sort of thing can happen. I should have been foxy, like Larkin or Revere, and faked a psychosis to stay out of the Army. This is where all my fucking prissy morality gets me—fucked!

What caps it off is this: The aged mediocrity before whom I am regularly brought for interviews has asked me to keep a record of my experience here. A journal. He says he admires the way I write! I have a real gift for words, this aged mediocrity says. Ye Gods!

For over a week I tried to behave like a proper prisoner of war—name, rank, and Social Security number—but it's like the hunger strike I attempted way back when in the Montgomery jail: People who can't diet four days running shouldn't attempt hunger strikes.

So here's your journal, aged asshole. You know what you can do with it.

June 3

He thanked me, that's what he did. He said, "I can understand that you find all this very upsetting, Mr. Sacchetti." (Mr. Sacchetti, yet!) "Believe me, we want to do everything in our power here at Camp Archimedes to make the transition easier. That's my Function. Your Function is to observe. To observe and interpret. But there's no need to start right away. It takes time to adjust to a new environment, I can certainly understand that. But I think I can safely say that once you have made that adjustment you'll enjoy your life here at Camp Archimedes far more than you would have enjoyed Springfield—or than you've enjoyed Springfield in the past. I've read the few notes you kept there, you know—"

I interrupted to say that I *didn't* know.

"Ah yes, Warden Smede was kind enough to send them along, and I read them. With great interest. In fact, it was only at my request that you were allowed to begin that journal. I wanted a sample of your work, so to speak, before I had you brought here.

"You really presented a very harrowing picture of your life in Springfield. I can honestly say I was shocked. I can assure you, Mr. Sacchetti, that *here* you'll suffer no such harassments. And there's none of that disgusting hanky-panky going on here either. I should think not! You were *wasting* yourself in that prison, Mr. Sacchetti. It was no place for a man of your intellectual attainments. I am myself something of an Expert in the R & D department. Not maybe what you'd call a Genius, exactly, I wouldn't go as far as that, but an Expert certainly."

"R & D?"

"Research and Development, you know. I have a nose for talent, and in my own small way, I'm rather well known. Inside the field. Haast is the name, Haast with a double A."

"Not *General* Haast?" I asked. "The one who took that Pacific island? My thought, of course, was that the Army had got me after all. (And for all I know that may yet be the case.)

He lowered his eyes to the surface of his desk. "Formerly, yes. But I'm rather too old now, as I believe you have yourself pointed out, eh?" Looking up resentfully: "Too *aged* . . . to remain in the Army." He pronounced *aged* as a single syllable.

"Though I have preserved a few Army ties, a circle of friends who still respect my opinion, aged as I am. I am surprised that *you* associate my name with Auaui . . . 1944 was rather before your time."

"But I read the book, and that came out in . . . when? . . . 1955." The book I referred to, as Haast knew at once, was Fred Berrigan's *Mars in Conjunction*, a very slightly fictionalized account of the Auaui campaign. Years after the book appeared I met Berrigan at a party. A splendid, intense fellow, but he seemed to be sweating doom. That was just a month before his suicide. All of which is another story.

Haast glowered. "I had a nose for talent in those days too. But talent sometimes goes hand in glove with treason. However, there is no point in discussing the Berrigan affair with you, as you've obviously made up your mind."

He returned then to the Welcome Wagon bit: I had the run of the library; I had a $50 weekly allowance (!) to spend at the canteen; movies on Tuesday and Thursday nights; coffee in the lounge; that sort of thing. Above all, I must feel free, feel free. He refused, as he always had before, to explain where I was, why I was there, or when I might expect to be released or sent back to Springfield.

"Just keep a good journal, Mr. Sacchetti. That's all we ask."

"Oh, you can call me Louie, General Haast."

"Why, thank you . . . Louie. And why don't you call me H.H.? All my friends do."

"H.H."

"Short for Humphrey Haast. But the name Humphrey has the wrong associations in these less liberal days. As I

13

was saying—your journal. Why don't you go back and fill in where you left off, when you were brought here. We want that journal to be as thoroughgoing as possible. Facts, Sacchetti—excuse me, Louie—*facts!* Genius, as the saying goes, is an infinite capacity for taking pains. Write it as though you were trying to explain to someone outside this . . . camp . . . what was happening to you. And I want you to be brutally honest. Say what you think. Don't spare *my* feelings."

"I'll try not to."

A wan smile. "But try and keep one principle in mind always. Don't become too, you know . . . obscure? Remember, what we want is facts. Not . . ." He cleared his throat.

"Poetry?"

"Personally, you understand, I have nothing against poetry. You're welcome to write as much of it as you like. In fact, do, do, by all means. You'll find an appreciative audience for poetry here. But in your journal you must try to make sense."

Fuck you, H.H.

(I must here interpose a childhood memory. When I was a paper boy, at about age thirteen, I had a customer on my route who was a retired Army officer. Thursday afternoon was collection day, and old Major Youatt would never pay up unless I came into his dim, mementoed living room and heard him out. There were two things he liked to soliloquize about: women and cars. On the first subject, his feelings were ambivalent; an itchy curiosity about my little girl friends alternated with oracular warnings about V.D. Cars he liked better: his eroticism was uncomplicated by fear. He kept pictures in his billfold of all the cars he had ever owned, and he would show them to me, tenderly gloating, an aged lecher caressing the trophies of past conquests. I have always suspected that the fact that I was twenty-nine years old before I learned to drive a car derived from my horror of this man.

The point of the anecdote is this—that Haast is the mirror image of Youatt. They are cut with the same template. The key word is *fitness.* I imagine Haast still does twenty push-ups in the morning and rides a few imaginary miles on his Exercycle. The wrinkly crust of his face is crisped to a tasty brown by a sun lamp. His sparse and graying hair is crew cut. He carries to an extreme the maniacal American credo that there is no death.

And he is probably a garden of cancers. Isn't that so, H.H.?)

Later:
I have succumbed. I went to the library (of Congress? it is *vast!*) and checked out some three dozen books, which now grace the shelves of my room. It is a room, not a cell at all: the door is left open day and night, if there can be said to be a day and night in this unwindowed, labyrinthine world. What the place lacks in windows it makes up for in doors: there are infinite recessions of white, Alphavillean hallways, punctuated with numbered doors, most of them locked. A regular Bluebeards castle. The only doors I found open were to rooms identical to mine, though apparently untenanted. Am I in the vanguard? A steady purr of air conditioners haunts the hallways and sings me to sleep at, as the saying goes, night. Is this some deep Pellucidar? Exploring the empty halls, I oscillated between a muted terror and a muted hilarity, as one does at a slightly unconvincing but not incompetent horror show.

My room (you want facts, you'll get facts):

> I love it. Look at how dark
> it is. One might almost call it stark.
> The white paint is no longer white.
> It is more like moonlight
> than like white paint.
> I almost faint,
> looking at it.
> I think it is yellow,
> but I am unable to say.

H.H. isnt going to be happy, I can tell. (Honestly, H.H., that just happened.) For instant poetry it doesn't quite come up to the level of "Ozymandias," but in all modesty I will be satisfied with less, yes.

15

My room (lets try it again):

Off-white (there's the difference, in brief, between fact and poesy); original abstract oil paintings on these off-white walls, in the impeccable corporate taste of the New York Hilton, paintings as neutral in content as blank walls or Rorschach cards; expensive Danish-mod slabs of cherrywood tricked out here and there with cheery, striped, cubical cushions; an Acrilan carpet in off-ocher; the supreme luxury of wasted space and empty corners. I would estimate that I have five hundred square feet of floor space. The bed is in its own little ell and can be screened from the main body of the room by vapid, flowery drapes. There is a feeling that all four off-white walls are of one-way glass, that every drooping milky globe of light masks a microphone.

What gives?

A question that is on the tip of every guinea pigs tongue.

The man who stocks the library has more exquisite taste than the interior decorator. For there was not one, not two, but three copies of *The Hills of Switzerland* on the shelf. Even, so help me God, a copy of *Gerard Winstanley, Puritan Utopist*. I read *Hills* through and was pleased to find no misprints, though the fetish poems had been put in the wrong order.

Still later:

I have been trying to read. I take up a book, but after a few paragraphs it loses my interest. One after another, I set aside Palgrave, Huizinga, Lowell, Wilenski, a chemistry text, Pascals *Provincial Letters*, and *Time* magazine. (We are, as I suspected, using tactical nuclear weapons now; two students were killed in a protest riot in Omaha.) I haven't felt a like restlessness since my sophomore year at Bard, when I changed my major three times in one semester.

The giddiness infects my whole body: There is a hollowness in my chest, a dryness in my throat, an altogether inappropriate inclination to laughter.

I mean, what's so funny?

June 4

A soberer morning-after.

As Haast requests, I will recount the events of the interim. May they be used in evidence against him.

The day after "The Silkworm Song"—that would be May 20—I was still sick and had remained in the cell while Donny and Peter (already reconciled) and the Mafia were out on a work detail. I was summoned to Smede's office to receive at his hand the package containing my personal effects. He made me check it item for item against the inventory that had been drawn up the day I'd entered prison. Searing blasts of hope, as I imagined that some miracle of public protest or judicial conscience had set me free. Smede shook my hand, and, delirious, I *thanked* him. Tears in my eyes. The son of a bitch must have been enjoying himself.

He handed me over then, with an envelope the same sickly yellow color as my prisoned flesh (this was the Sacchetti dossier, surely) two guards in black uniforms, trimmed in silver, very Germanic and, as we used to say, tuff. Calf-high boots, leather straps that formed a veritable harness, mirror sunglasses, the works: Peter would have groaned with envy, Donny with desire. They said not a word but went straight to their work. Handcuffs. A limousine with curtains. I sat between them and asked questions of their stone faces and shielded eyes. An airplane. Sedation. And so, by a route unmarked even by bread crumbs, to my comfy little cell in Camp Archimedes, where the witch feeds me very good meals. (I have only to ring a bell for room service.)

I arrived here, I'm told, the twenty-second. First interview with H.H. the next day. Warm reassurances and obstinate mystifications. As noted, I remained noncommunicative until the second of June. Those nine days passed in an Empyrean of paranoia, but that, like all passions, ebbed,

17

diminished to an ordinary humdrum horror, thence to an uneasy curiosity. Shall I confess that there is a kind of pleasure to be had in the situation, that a strange castle *is* rather more interesting than the same old dungeon all the time?

But confess it to whom? To H.H.? To Louis II, whom I must confront in the mirror almost every day now?

No, I shall pretend that this journal is just for me. My journal. If Haast wants a copy, Haast will have to supply me with carbon paper.

Later:
I wonder, reading over "The Silkworm Song," if the fifth line is quite right. I want an effect of disingenuous pathos; perhaps I've achieved no more than a cliché.

June 5

Haast informs me, by inter-office memo, that the electric typewriter I use is part of a master-slave hookup that automatically produces, in another room, second, third, and fourth impressions of everything I type. H.H. gets his *Journal* fresh off the press—and think of all the money he saves not having to supply me with carbon paper.

Today, the first evidence that there is that here which merits chronicling:

On the way to the library to get tapes to play on my hi-fi (a B & O, no less) I encountered one of the spirits inhabiting this circle of my new hell, the first circle, if I am to go through them in a proper, Dantean order— Limbo—and he, stretching the analogy a bit further, would be the Homer of this dark glade.

Dark it was, for the fluorescent fixtures had been removed from this length of corridor, and as in a glade a constant and chill wind swept through the pure Euclidean space, some anomaly in the ventilating system, I suppose. He stood there blocking my way, his face buried in his hands, corn silk–white hair twined about the nervous fingers, swaying and, I think, whispering to himself. I approached quite close, but he did not rouse from his meditation, so I spoke aloud: "Hello there."

· And when even this drew no response, I ventured further. "I'm new here. I was a prisoner at Springfield, a conchie. I've been brought here illegally. Though God knows to what purpose."

He took his hands from his face and looked at me, squint-eyed, through the tangled hair. A broad, young face, Slavic and guileless—like one of the second-string heroes in an Eisenstein epic. The broad lips broadened in a chill, unconvinced smile, like a stage moonrise. He lifted his right hand and touched the center of my chest with three fingers, as though to assure himself of my corporeality. Assured, the smile became more convinced.

"Do you know," I asked urgently, "where we are? Or what's to be done with us?"

The pale eyes looked from side to side—in confusion or fear, I could not tell.

"What city? what state?"

Again, that wintry smile of recognition, as my words bridged the long distance to his understanding. "Well, the nearest any of us can tell, we're in the mountain states. Because of *Time,* you know." He pointed to the magazine in my hand. He spoke in the most nasal of Midwestern voices, in an accent unmodified by education or travel. He was in speech as in looks a model Iowa farmboy.

"Because of *Time?*" I asked, somewhat confused. I looked at the face on the cover (General Phee Phi Pho Phum of North Malaysia, or some other yellow peril), as though *he* might explain.

"It's a regional edition. *Time* comes out in different regional editions. For advertising purposes. And *we* get the mountain states edition. The mountain states are Idaho, Utah, Wyoming, Colorado . . ." He named their names as though twanging chords on a guitar.

"Ah! Yes, I understand now. Slow of me."

He heaved a deep sigh.

I held out my hand, which he regarded with undisguised reluctance. (There are parts of the country, the West Coast especially, where because of the germ warfare the

19

handshake is no longer considered good form.) "The name's Sacchetti. Louis Sacchetti."

"Ah! Ah yes!" He took hold of my hand convulsively. "Mordecai said you were coming. I'm *so* glad to meet you. I can't express—" He broke off, blushing deeply, and pulled his hand out of mine. "Wagner," he mumbled, as if an afterthought. "George Wagner." Then, with a certain bitterness, "But *you* would never have heard of me."

I've encountered this particular form of introduction so often at readings or symposia, from other little-magazine writers or teaching assistants, smaller fry even than myself, that my response was almost automatic. "No, I'm afraid I haven't, George. Sorry to say. I'm surprised, as a matter of fact, that you've heard of *me*."

George chuckled. "He's surprised . . ." he drawled, "as a matter of fact . . . that I've heard of *him!*"

Which was no little disconcerting.

George closed his eyes. "Excuse me," he said, almost whispering. "The light. The light is too bright."

"This Mordecai that you mentioned . . . ?"

"I like to come here because of the wind. I can breathe again. Breathing the wind. Here." Or perhaps what he said was "hear," for he went on: "If you're very quiet you can hear their voices."

I was indeed very quiet, but the only sound was the sea-shell roaring of the air conditioners, the gloomy blasts of chill air through the chambered corridor.

"Whose voices?" I asked with a certain trepidation.

George furrowed his white brows. "Why, the angels, of course."

Mad, I thought—and then realized that George had been quoting my own poem to me—the paraphrase-cum-parody I'd done of the Duino Elegies. That George, this ingenuous Iowa boy, should so lightly toss off a line from one of my uncollected poems was even more disconcerting than the simpler supposition that he was off his nut. "You've read that poem?" I asked.

George nodded and the tangle of corn silk crept down over pale eyes, as though from shyness.

"It isn't a very good poem."

"No, I suppose not." George's hands, which had till now been preoccupied with each other behind his back, began

20

to creep back up to George's face. They reached up to push the drooping hair back from his eyes, then stayed atop his head, as though snared. "But it's true anyhow . . . you *can* hear their voices. Voices of silence. Or the breath, it's the same thing. Mordecai says that breath is poetry too." The hands slowly came down in front of the pale eyes.

"Mordecai?" I repeated, with some urgency. I could not then, I still cannot, shake off the feeling that I've heard that name elsewhere, elsewhen.

But it was like speaking to someone in a boat that the current was ineluctably bearing away. George shuddered. "Go away," he whispered. "Please."

But I did not, not at once, go away. I stood there before him, though he seemed to have become quite oblivious of me. Gently he rocked back and forth, from his heels to the balls of his feet, then back on his heels. His fine hair stirred in the steady, hissing exhalation from the ventilator.

He spoke aloud to himself, but I could only catch a little of what he said. "Linkages of light, corridors, stairways . . ." The words had a familiar ring, but I could not place them. "Spaces of being and shields of bliss."

Abruptly he took his hands from his face and stared at me. "Are you still there?" he asked.

And though the answer was self-evident, I said that, yes, I was still here.

In the semidarkness of the corridor his irises had dilated, and it was this perhaps that made him seem so sad. Again he laid three fingers on my chest. "Beauty," he said solemnly, "is nothing but the beginning of a terror that we are able barely to endure." And with those words George Wagner heaved up the entirety of a considerable breakfast into that pure Euclidean space. Almost at once the guards were about us, a brood of black mother hens, giving George a mouth rinse, mopping up, and conducting us our separate ways. They gave me something to drink too. A tranquilizer, I suspect; else, I should not have the presence of mind yet to document the encounter.

What a strange fellow he was though! A farmboy quoting Rilke. Farmboys might recite Whittier perhaps, or even Carl Sandburg. But the *Duinoser Elegien?*

21

June 6

ROOM 34

Stolid stainless-steel numbers pasted to a prosaic blond-wood door, and beneath, in white letters graven on a rectangle of black plastic (like those that show a bank teller's name on one side and NEXT WINDOW PLEASE on the other):

DR. A. BUSK

My guards led me within and entrusted me to the severe tutelage of the two chairs, which, webs of black leather slung from bands of chromed steel, were but the abstractions—an attar, as it were—of the guards themselves. Chairs by Harley-Davidson. Hard-edge paintings (chosen for the pleasures of such chairs) flattened themselves against the walls, yearning to become invisible.

Dr. A. Busk strides into the room and threatens me with her hand. Am I to shake it? No, she is only motioning me to be seated. I am seated, she is seated, crossing her legs, snick-snack, pulling at the hem of her skirt, smiling. It is a credible if not a kindly smile, a little too thin, too crisp. The high, clear brow, and retricent eyebrows of an Elizabethan noblewoman. Forty years old? More likely forty-five.

"Excuse me if I do not offer you my hand, Mr. Sacchetti, but we'll get on much better if we dispense with that kind of hypocrisy from the beginning. It's not as though you were spending your vacation here, is it? You are a prisoner, and I am . . . what? I am the prison. That's the beginning of an honest, if not altogether pleasant, relationship."

"By honest do you mean that I shall be allowed to insult *you* as well?"

"With impunity, Mr. Sacchetti. Tit for tat. Either here

22

or at your leisure, in your journal. I am sent the second copy, so you can be certain that anything unpleasant you have to say will not be in vain."

"I'll keep it in mind."

"Meanwhile, there are a few things you should know about what we are doing here. Yesterday you met young Wagner, but in your journal you pointedly refrained from any kind of speculation concerning his rather remarkable behavior. Though you certainly must have given the matter some thought."

"I certainly must have."

Dr. A. Busk pursed her lips and tapped a ragged fingernail on the envelope clipped to her clipboard—the Sacchetti dossier again. *"Do* let's be candid, Mr. Sacchetti. It must have occurred to you that young George's behavior was not wholly consistent, and you must also have associated these inconsistencies with certain remarks concerning your role here that my colleague, Mr. Haast, has let drop. Not, I may point out, accidentally. You must, in short, have come to suspect that young George is the subject—one of the subjects—in an experimental program that is being carried out here?" She raised a reticent, questioning eyebrow. I nodded.

"You could not have guessed—and perhaps it will ease your mind to learn?—that young George is here voluntarily. You see, he deserted the Army while on furlough in Taipei. The usual sordid sort of thing with a soldier and a prostitute. Of course he was found and court-marshaled. His sentence was five years imprisonment, a mild sentence, you must admit. Had we been officially at war, he might have been shot. Yes, quite likely."

"Then it *is* the Army that's kidnapped me?"

"Not exactly. Camp Archimedes is operated under a grant from a private foundation, though to preserve the necessary secrecy we are quite autonomous. Only one officer of the foundation knows the exact nature of our research. For the rest of them—and for the Army—we come under that all-inclusive category of weapons development. A good many of the personnel—most of the guards, and I myself—have been borrowed, as it were, from the Armed Services."

With that knowledge, all her attributes—the scrubbed face, the stiff manner, the defeminized voice—coalesced into a viable image: "You're a WAC!"

In reply she made an ironic salute. "So, as I was saying, poor George went to the brig, and he wasn't happy there. He could not, as my colleague, Mr. Haast, is wont to say, adjust to a brig environment. When the opportunity came for him to volunteer for Camp Archimedes he leaped at it. After all, *most* experiments these days are in the field of immunology. Some of the new diseases are extremely unpleasant. That's young George's story. The other subjects you will meet have analogous backgrounds."

"This subject doesn't."

"You are not, precisely, a subject. But to understand just why you've been brought here, you must first understand the purpose of the experiment. It is an investigation of learning processes. I need not explain to you the fundamental importance of education with respect to the national defense effort. Ultimately it is intelligence that is a nation's most vital resource, and education can be seen as the process of maximizing intelligence. However, as such it is almost invariably a failure, since this primary purpose is sacrificed to the purpose of socialization. When intelligence *is* maximized, it is almost always at the expense of the socialization process—I might cite your own case in this respect—and so, from society's point of view, little has been gained. A cruel dilemma.

"It is perhaps the chief mission of the science of psychology to resolve this dilemma—to maximize intelligence without vitiating its social utility. I hope that's clear?"

"Cicero himself had not so pure a Latin style."

La Busk crinkled her high, unpenciled brows, not getting the point, then, deciding it wasn't worth her while to pursue it, mere a-social levity, unfurrowed and continued:

"And therefore we are exploring certain new educational techniques here, techniques of adult education. In an adult, the socializing process has been completed. Few subjects exhibit marked character development after age twenty-five. Therefore, if the process of intelligence maximization can be initiated then—if the stultified creative faculties can be reawakened, so to speak—then we may

24

begin to exploit that most precious resource, the mind, as it has never been exploited before.

"Unhappily we have been given what amount to defective materials to work with. When one must rely upon Army brigs for experimental subjects, one introduces a systematic error into the work, since for such people the process of socialization was clearly unsuccessful. And to be quite candid, it's *my* opinion that this error in selection is already having its unhappy consequences. I hope you note that down in your journal.

I assured her that I would. I couldn't refrain then—little as I wanted to give her the satisfaction of seeing how much she had picqued my curiosity—from asking: "By new educational techniques, am I to assume you mean drugs?"

"Ah ha. Then you have been giving the matter some thought. Yes, certainly, drugs. Though not in the sense you perhaps suppose. There are, as any college freshman these days knows, drugs available from extralegal sources that can temporarily assist memory retention by as much as two hundred per cent, or speed up other learning processes proportionately. But the learning curves flatten out with continued use of such drugs, and one soon reaches the point of diminishing returns, and finally no returns at all. There are such drugs, and there are others too, such as LSD, which can produce a specious sense of omniscience. I needn't tell *you* of such drugs though, need I, Mr. Sacchetti?"

"Is *that* down on my profile? I must say you've been thorough."

"Oh, there's very little we don't know about you, sir. Before you were brought here you may be sure we examined every dirty little cranny of your past. It wouldn't do to bring just any conchie here, you know. We had to be certain you were harmless. We know you inside and out. Your schools, relatives, friends, what you've read, where you've been. We know what room you occupied in every hotel you stayed at in Switzerland and Germany when you had your Fulbright. We know every girl you dated at Bard and afterward, and just how far you got with each. And it hasn't been a very good showing, I

25

must say. We know, in considerable detail, just how much you've earned during the last fifteen years, and how you've spent it. Any time the government cares to, it can send you right back to Springfield on tax evasion charges. We have the records from your two years of psycho-therapy."

"And have you bugged the confessionals as well?"

"Only since you came to Springfield. That's how we found out about your wife's abortion and your nasty little affair with that Miss Webb."

"Good-looking though, wasn't she?"

"If you like weak types. But to get back to business . . . your task here is quite simple. You will be allowed to circulate among the subjects, to speak with them, to share, as far as possible, their day-to-day life. And to report, in brief compass, the matters with which they are preoccupied, their amusements, and your own estimation of the . . . what shall I say? . . . of the intellectual climate here. I suspect you will enjoy the work."

"Perhaps. But why me?"

"One of the subjects recommended you. Of the various candidates we considered, you seemed most apt for the work—and certainly the most available. In all honesty it must be said that we have been having . . . communica-tions problems with the subjects. And it was their ring-leader—Mordecai Washington his name is—who suggested that you be brought here to act as a sort of go-between, an interpreter. Do you remember Mordecai? He went to the same high school you did for one year, '55."

"Central High School? The name seems vaguely fa-miliar, but I can't place it. I may have heard it read off some attendance sheet, but he certainly wasn't a friend. I never had so many that I'm apt to forget their names."

"You'll have ample opportunity to repair that omission here then. Are there any more questions?"

"Yes. What does the A. stand for?"

She looked blank.

"In *Dr. A. Busk*," I clarified.

"Oh, that. It stands for Aimée."

"And which private foundation is supplying the cash for this place?"

"I could tell you, but really, Mr. Sacchetti, don't you

think you'd be better off not knowing? The subjects have been instructed that there are certain things which, for your own sake, it would be better that they not discuss with you. Because you will, I presume, want to leave here sometime, won't you?"

Dr. Aimée Busk uncrossed her legs with a slither of nylon and stood up. "The guards will be here directly to take you back upstairs. I shall see you again next week at the latest. In the meantime, feel free to come and ask me any question that you're certain you want to have the answer to. Good day, Mr. Sacchetti." With three brisk scissor steps she left the room. Having scored all the points for *that* round.

Later:
Within an hour after I'd typed this journal entry, a note came from H.H.: "She's thirty-seven. H.H."

Interdepartmental rivalries? (Don't answer that question.)

June 7

I had thought my migraines, being so clearly psychosomatic, had been exorcised by my psychotherapy, but they returned last night with a vengeance. Where one twinge had been there now are seven. Perhaps La Busk, being an initiate to the mysteries, was able to work some countermagic to Dr. Mieris's cure; perhaps it was simply that I stayed up past two o'clock in a fit of scribbling. I don't yet have enough distance from it to judge whether the poem was worth such a price. Though who knows? Perhaps it was the migraine brought on the poem.

So much for the life of the mind; the notable event of the day was the visitation, shortly after breakfast (at noon) of the fabled Mordecai Washington. He came unannounced by any guard, knocked but didn't wait to be invited in. "May I?" he asked, having already done so.

Even face to face, even with his voice, his loud voice, thudding against my migraine, I did not recognize him as my supposed high school friend, as anyone.

A first impression: He is not good-looking. I'll admit my standards of beauty are ethnocentric, but I don't think many Negroes would find Mordecai Washington good-looking either. Very dark he is, well-nigh purplish. Long in the face, with a jaw that juts and blub lips (flattened against the plane of the face, however, rather than protruding; vertical lips, one might call them), a minimal nose, and tousley neo-Maori hair. A chest that would a century past have been called consumptive, negligible shoulders, bandy legs, clodhopper feet. A gravelly rasp of a voice, like Punch in a puppet show. Handsome eyes, however (though it's always easy to concede that to ugly people).

Even so, I will insist that he has extraordinary eyes, at once moist and lively, suggesting depths but never revealing them, oxymoronal eyes.

"No, stay where you are," he insisted, when I began to climb out of bed. He dragged a chair across the room to my bedside. "What are you reading? Ah, a picture book. You've been here all this while, and no one told me. I found out from George. It's a pity, but then I've been temporarily"—He waved a hand above his head vaguely. (His hands, like his feet, were disproportionately big. Fingers splayed at the tips like a workman's, but quick, almost fluttery. His gestures tend to be overdramatic, as though to compensate for his deadpan face.)—"defunct. Inert. Moribund. Comatose. But that's all over now. And you're here. I'm glad. I am. Mordecai Washington."

Gravely, he offered me his hand. I could not help sensing a certain irony in this gesture, as though in accepting it I was serving as his straight man.

He laughed, shrill parrot laughter pitched two octaves higher than his speaking voice. It was as though another person did his laughing for him. "Oh, you can touch it. I won't give you any goddamn germs. Not that way, boss."

"It hadn't even occurred to me . . . Mordecai." (I have never been able to use first names with strangers readily.)

"Oh, I didn't expect you'd remember me. Don't feel bad on that account. And you don't have to tutoyer me, yet." This, in abysmal French. "But I've remembered you. Eidetically, the way you remember a particular moment from a horror movie. *Psycho,* for instance? Remember *Psycho?*"

"Yes, the shower sequence. Was I like Tony Perkins in those days? God forbid."

"You were terrifying enough in your own way. To me. We were in the same homeroom. Miss Squinlin, remember her?"

"Miss Squinlin! Yes, I hated that woman."

"Fat old red-faced cunt—I hated her a hell of a lot more than you ever did, brother. I had her for English 10-C. *Silas Marner, Julius Caesar, Rime of the Ancient Mariner.* Jesus Christ, I almost stopped speaking the fucking language, she made me hate it so."

"You still haven't explained what I had in common with *Psycho.*"

"Well, let's say *Donovan's Brain* instead. A brain in a glass tank. The Octopus intellect sniffling off after scholarships, knowing all the answers, devouring all the shit that the Squinlins could shovel in. The cerebrum as Cerberus." He spoiled the cleverness of this by mispronouncing both words.

"And when you wanted to, you could put *down* people like old Squinlin. Me, I just had to sit there and take their shit. I knew it was shit, but what could I do? They had me coming and going.

"The thing about you that's really stuck in my mind— hell, it changed my life!—was one day in the spring of '55, you and a couple of those Jewish broads you hung around with were staying after school yakking away about whether or not there was a Gaud. That's what you called him— Gaud. You had a real fakey accent then—from seeing too many Laurence Olivier movies, I'll bet. I was sitting at the back of the room on detention. Sullen and invisible, as was my way. Does any of it come back?"

"Not that particular day. I talked a lot about Gaud that year. I had just discovered the Enlightenment, as it's called. I remember the two girls though. Barbara—and who was the other one?"

"Ruth."

"What a fearful memory you have."

29

"The better to eat you with, my darling. Anyhow, to get back—the two broads would bring up those hoary arguments about the universe is like a watch, and you can't have a watch without a watchmaker. Or the first cause, that no other causes causes. Till that day I'd never even heard the watchmaker bit, and when they came out with it, I thought, Now, *that'll* stop old Donovan's Brain. But not a bit of it—you just tore their sappy syllogisms"— another foul mispronunciation—"to pieces. They never got the message, they just kept coming on with the same old crap—but I did. You toppled me right out of that old-time religion."

"I'm sorry, Mordecai. Truly I am. One never realizes how many other lives we can poison with what we think is our own error. I don't know how—"

"Sorry? Baby, I was *thanking* you. It may seem a strange way to do it, having you hijacked to this hole-in-the-ground, but it's a better life you'll lead here than you led in Springfield. Haast showed me the journal you were keeping there. You're well out of it. But I'll admit it wasn't *only* altruism made me ask Haast to bring you here. It was my big chance to meet a first-class, bonafide, published poet. You really went the whole way, didn't you, Sacchetti?" Impossible to sort out the feelings he mingled in that one question: admiration, contempt, envy, and—which affected nearly everything Mordecai said to me—a sort of haughty mirth.

"I take it that you've read *The Hills of Switzerland?*" I returned. Trust a writer's vanity to take the first opportunity to sneak that in!

Mordecai shrugged his negligible shoulders. "Yeah. I read it."

"Then you know that I've outgrown the callow materialism of those days. God exists quite independently of Aquinas. Faith is more than a mastery of syllogisms."

"Fuck faith, and fuck your epigrams. You're not my Big Brother any more. I'm two years *your* senior, friend. And as for your latter-day piety, I had you brought here *despite* that, and despite some stinking awful poetry too."

What could I do but flinch?

Mordecai smiled, his anger bevanished as soon as ex-

30

ON-THE-FLY ITEM

SEND TO TECH
SERVICES

pressed. "There were some stinking good poems too. George liked the book as a whole better than I did, and George knows more about such things. For one thing, he's been here longer. What'd you think of him?"

"Of George? He was . . . very intense. I'm afraid I wasn't quite prepared for so much all at once. I'm afraid I'm still not. You're pretty fast and loose down here, especially after the total vacuum of Springfield."

"Like hell. What's your I.Q. anyhow?"

"Does it make sense, at my age, to talk about I.Q.'s? In '57 I scored a hundred and sixty on one test, but I don't know how far along the standard curve that would take me. But *now* what difference does a printed test make? It's a question entirely of what you *do* with your intelligence."

"I know—ain't it a bitch?" Lightly as he tossed this off, I felt that I had for the first time in our talk touched a theme that Mordecai regarded with any sort of seriousness.

"What *are* you doing, Mordecai? Here, in this place. And what is this place? What are Haast and Busk trying to get out of you people?"

"This is hell, Sacchetti, didn't you know? Or its antechamber. They're trying to buy our souls up so they can use our bodies for sausages."

"They told you that I shouldn't know anything about it—is that it?"

Mordecai faced away from me and walked across the room to the bookshelf. "We're geese, and into our gullets Haast and Busk are stuffing Western Culture. Science, art, philosophy, whatever can be crammed in. And still . . .

> I am not full, I am not full.
> My stomach has been flushed and flushed,
> and yet I cannot hold
> my food, I cannot touch   Oh!
> I am not full."

It was my own poem that Mordecai had quoted. My reaction wavered between the flattery I felt at his having singled out just that passage to memorize (for it is one I

31

am most proud of) and a pity for the poignance of what
he had said, not less poignant for my having said it first. I
made no reply, asked no more questions.

Mordecai dropped leadenly onto the couch. "This room
is a fucking mess, Sacchetti. All our rooms were like this
at the start, but you don't have to put up with it. Tell
Haast you want something classier. Say the curtains inter-
fere with your brain waves. We've got carte blanche here
for things like interior decoration—as you'll see. So take
advantage of it."

"Compared to Springfield this seems quite elegant. For
that matter, compared to anywhere I've ever lived, barring
a single day at the Ritz."

"Yeah, poets don't make so damn much money, do
they? I'll bet I was a lot better off than you—before I got
drafted. The motherfuckers. That was a big mistake, getting drafted."

"You arrived at Camp Archimedes the same way
George did, via the brig?"

"Yeah. Assaulting an officer. The son of a bitch kept
asking for it. They all keep asking for it, but they never
get it. Well, that son of a bitch did. I knocked the
mother's teeth out, two of them. Bad scene. The brig was
a worse scene—they're really down on you after a thing
like that. So I volunteered. That was six, seven months
back. Sometimes I think maybe it wasn't such a big mistake. I'll say this for the stuff they gave us—it beats acid.
With acid you *think* you know everything. With this, you
goddamn well do. But it isn't so often I can get as high as
all that. Most of the time it's a pain. Like H.H. says:
'Genius is an infinite capacity for pain.' "

I laughed, as much from sheer dizziness at the speed
and shifts of his rhetoric as in appreciation of the *mot*.

"But it *was* a mistake. I was better off dumb."

"Dumb? It doesn't sound like that was ever exactly
your condition."

"I sure as hell never had no hundred and sixty I.Q. Not
this mother."

"Oh, but those tests are gimmicked for middle-class
WASPs like me. Or I suppose I should say WASCs. Mea-
suring intelligence isn't as simple as taking a blood sample."

"Thanks for saying so, but the truth is I *was* a dumb

son of a bitch. And even more ignorant than dumb. Everything that I know now, the way I'm talking with you—it's all on account of the Pa—on account of the stuff they gave me."

"All of it? No."

"Fucking *all* of it!" He laughed, a calmer laugh than at first "It's gratifying to talk with you, Sacchetti. You flinch at my every obscenity."

"Do I! It's that middle-class upbringing, I suppose. I'm well used to the Anglo-Saxon words in print, but somehow the spoken word . . . it's a reflex."

"That picture book you're looking at—have you read the text that goes with it?"

I had been browsing through the second volume of Wilenski's *Flemish Painters*, which contains the plates. Volume One is all text. "I started to, but I got bogged down. I haven't settled down enough to be able to concentrate on anything."

Mordecai's reaction to this seemed unduly grave. He said nothing in response, however, but after a pause continued his first train of thought. "There's a passage in there that's terrific. Can I read it to you?" He'd already taken Volume One down from the shelf. "It's about Hugo van der Goes. You know about him?"

"Only that he was one of the earliest Flemish painters. I don't think I've seen anything of his though."

"You couldn't have. None of it survived. Nothing that he signed, at any rate. The story goes that around 1470 he went mad, raved about being damned and the devil was going to get him and all that. He was already living in this monastery near Brussels at the time, and the brothers would play music to try and calm him, like David with Saul. One of the boys there wrote an account of his madness—its all worth reading—but the part of it I really liked . . . here, let me read it to you.

" '. . . Brother Hugo from inflaming of his imaginative powers was disposed to daydreaming fantasies and hallucination and suffered in consequence an illness of the brain. For there is, I am told, a small delicate organ, near the brain, which is controlled by the creative and imaginative powers. If our imagination is too vivid or our fantasy too abundant, this little organ is affected, and if it is strained to the breaking point madness or frenzy results. If we are to avoid falling into this irremediable' "—

Mordecai faltered pronouncing this word

—" 'danger, we must limit our fantasy, our imaginations, and our suspicions and exclude all other vain and useless thoughts which may excite our brains. We are all but men, and the disaster that fell upon our Brother as a result of his fantasies and hallucinations, could it not also fall on us?' "

"Isn't that great? I can just imagine the old bastard, the satisfaction he got writing it down—'I told you so, Hugo! Didn't I always say that all that painting was *dangerous?*' Why do you suppose he did go mad, though?"

"Anyone can go mad. It's not the prerogative of painters. Or poets."

"Yeah, I suppose when you come right down to it, everybody's crazy. My folks were sure enough crazy. Mammy—that's what we called her, so help me!—Mammy was crazy with the holy ghost, and the old man was crazy without it. Both my brothers were junkies, so that makes them crazy. Crazy and crazy and crazy and crazy."

"Is something wrong?" I asked, rising from bed and going toward Mordecai, who had become increasingly agitated during this speech, until at last, trembling, eyes pressed tightly closed, one hand upon his heart, his speech degenerated into a mere static of choked breath. The heavy book dropped from his left hand to the floor, and at its impact he opened his eyes. "I'll be . . . all right if I . . . sit down a minute. A little dizzy."

I helped him back to the sofa and, lacking a better remedy, brought him a glass of water, which he drank gratefully. His hands, holding the glass, still trembled.

"And yet, you know . . ." he resumed quietly, running his spatulate fingers up and down the flutings of the glass, "there was something about van der Goes. At least I like to think there was. Something special about any artist, of course. A sort of magic—in the literal sense. Unriddling

34

the signatures of nature, and breathing the same secrets back. It's like that isn't it?"

"I don't know. I don't think it's that for me, but there are many artists who would *like* it to be like that. But the problem with magic is that it doesn't work."

"Like hell," Mordecai said quietly.

"Can you scoff at God and believe in demons?"

"What are demons? I believe in elemental powers— sylphs, salamanders, undines, gnomes—parables of primal matter. You smile and sneer and cuddle up in the comfortable Jesuitical universe of College Physics. Matter has no mysteries left for you, oh no! No more than the spirit does. All tidy and known, like a mother's cooking. Well, ostriches feel at home in the universe too, though they can't see it."

"Believe me, Mordecai, I'd be happy in a world of sylphs and salamanders. Any poet would. What do you think we've all been bellyaching about these past two hundred years? We've been evicted.

"But you still sneer at the words. For you they're nothing but a Russian ballet, a tinkle of bells. But I have *seen* the salamanders, dwelling in the midst of flames."

"Mordecai! The very notion that flame is an element is nonsense. Half a semester of chemistry would disabuse you of that idea. High school chemistry, at that."

"Flame is the element of change," he said, in an exalted, orgulous tone, "of the transubstantial. It's the bridge between matter and spirit. What else is it lives in the heart of your giant cyclotrons? Or at the heart of the sun? You believe in angels, don't you—the mediaries between this and the farthest sphere? Well, I have *spoken* with them."

"The farthest sphere—that which God inhabits?"

"Gaud, Gaud! I prefer familiar spirits—my sylphs and salamanders—who will answer when spoken to. Two in the hand are worth one in the bush. But there's no use our arguing. Not yet. Wait till you've seen my laboratory. Unless we adjust our vocabularies for mutual comprehension, we'll go on oscillating between Sic and Non till fucking doomsday."

"I'm sorry—I'm not usually so inflexible. I imagine it's a matter less of reasoned dissent than of mental self-preservation. It would be easy to let myself be swept up in your rhetoric. That's meant to be a compliment, you know."

"It bugs you, doesn't it, that I'm smarter than you are?"

"Didn't it bug you, Mordecai, when the tables were turned, when you knew me first? Besides"—smiling, trying to put a good face on the matter—"I'm not sure you are."

"Oh, I am, I am. Believe me. Or test me, if you'd like. Any time. Just name your weapon, baby. Pick a science, any science. Maybe a formal debate would suit you better? Do you know the dates of the reigns of the kings of England, France, Spain, Sweden, Prussia? A scramble up the slopes of *Finnegan's Wake* perhaps? Haikus?"

"Stop! I believe you. But goddamn it, there's still *one* field that I'd win in yet, superman."

Mordecai tossed his head back defiantly. "What's that?"

"Orthoepy."

"Okay, I'll bite. What's orthoepy?"

"The study of correct pronunciation."

Lucifer, falling from heaven, was not so dismayed. "Yeah, yeah, that's so. But damn it, I don't have the *time* to look up and see how every dinky word is pronounced. But when I say a thing the wrong way, will you correct me?"

"I suppose a poet should be good for that, if nothing else."

"Oh, there's a lot that we've got lined up for you. You'll have to talk with George again. Not today, he's in sick bay today. He has some great ideas for putting on *Doctor Faustus* here, but we've been waiting till you were around. And there's one other thing too . . . ?" Uncharacteristically, Mordecai seemed unsure of his ground.

"And that?"

"I've written something. A story. I thought you could read it and tell me what you think. Haast has promised I can send it out to a magazine, after N.S.A. has checked it out. But I'm not sure it's good enough. I mean, in an absolute sense. Everybody *here* likes it, but we've become an awfully tight little group. Inbred. You've still got your own head on your shoulders though."

"I'd be glad to read it, and I assure you I'll be as nasty a critic as I know how. What's it about?"

"About? Jesus Christ, that's a hell of a question to get from a poet. It's about van der Goes, as a matter of fact."

"And what is N.S.A.?"

"National Security Agency. The code boys. They check over everything we say—it all goes down on tape, you know—to make sure we're not being . . . hermetic."

"Are you being hermetic?"

Mordecai, the alchemist, winked. "Abracadabra," he said meaningfully. Then, quick as a sylph, he was gone.

Later:

In summary? As easily summarize a tiltawhirl.

Guilt certainly, for having been the agent of Mordecai's falling-away. It never ceases to amaze how far-reaching an effect our slightest actions may have. The monk in his cloister entertains an error, imagining the danger to be only his, but a century hence his heresy may have convulsed nations. Perhaps the conservatives are right, perhaps free thought *is* dangerous.

But how the Old Adam, Louie II, protests at that! Do what I will, I can never quite silence him. It takes all the force of volition, at times, to prevent *his* voice from speaking aloud. He is always waiting, crouched in my heart, to usurp the sovereignty of reason.

But guilt is only a small part of what I feel. Wonder and awe, much more. Like some watcher of the skies/ When a new planet swims into his ken. The morning star. Lucifer, prince of darkness. Tempter.

June 8

Zu viel, zu viel! I have been all the day talking, talking. My mind is a 33 record being played at 78. I've met all but three or four of the score that are here; among themselves the prisoners are even more daunting than taken singly. The resonances of those many meetings still

37

swell up within me, like reminiscences of music after the opera.

It began early, when a guard brought me an ink-damp invitation to visit George W. in the sick bay, than which no hospital, not Wren's Chelsea, could be more magnificent. His bed might have been by Tiepolo. And flowers by the Douanier Rousseau. We talked more of Rilke, whom George admires less for his craft than for his heretic notions. He's done his own translations. Eccentric prosody. I reserved judgment. Discussed his ideas for staging *Faustus*, which led to his project for a model theater. It is to be *built* for him down here! (There is no longer any question but that Camp A. is deep underground.)

I can't remember the names of all the others, or all that was said. Only one, Murray Something-or-Other, an overfine young fellow with a porcelain manner, did I take a decided dislike to, which he reciprocated (though I may be flattering myself; more likely he didn't even know I was there). He led a fiery discussion of alchemical jabberwock. Which I would paraphrase so: "Two cocks coupling in darkness; from their brood are hatched dragontailed chicks. In seven times seven days these are burned, their ashes triturated in vessels of sacred lead." To which I say: Pish! But how earnestly they regarded his pish! As I later confirmed, this preoccupation has been largely Mordecai's doing.

Who I liked best was Barry Meade. I'm always pleased to meet people fatter than myself. Meade is hung up on movies, and at two o'clock, when George had to be sedated for his nap (poor George is in bad shape, but everyone I asked seems to have a different notion of the cause), he took me to the little projection room three levels down and showed me a montage he has made of McNamara's policy speeches and screaming women, clipped out of old horror movies. Hilarity mounting to hysteria. Barry, very cool, kept apologizing for imperceptible nuances of error.

4:30: George was awake again, but he ignored me for a math book. I begin to have the feeling that like a child visiting childless relatives for a holiday, the responsibility for my entertainment is being parceled out among them.

It happened in the afternoon, at least, that I came under the care of one who was introduced to me simply as "the Bishop." I suspect it is his dandified clothes earned him the nickname. He exposited the social order that has evolved here. In brief, it stands thus: that Mordecai, by main strength and charisma, is the unchallenged czar of a benevolent anarchy. The Bishop comes to Camp A. not out of the brig but from an Army mental hospital, where he had been two years suffering from total amnesia. He made a fascinating, droll, and scary recital of his multiple suicide attempts. He once drank a whole quart of lead paint. Yech.

Later on, he walloped me at chess.

Still later on, Murray Something-or-Other played electronic music. (His own? Somebody said yes, someone else said no.) In my manic condition even that sounded good.

And more. And more. Ossa on Pelion.

Too much, I'll say it again. And what is to come of it all? Why was this splendid monster given life? Tune in tomorrow.

June 9

Ah, but its one of *those* tomorrows—the sort when I feel that entropy is winning. I feel, on this tomorrow, as hollow as a papier-mâché mask, all grin and wink and wrinkle. The truth perhaps—the *true* truth—is not so much that the mask is hollow as that I don't care to look behind it at the nystagmic flicker of image image image that the nethermind is broadcasting to the faulty receptor of the overmind. I am bad and silly and defeated today. I am sick.

There were visitors—Mordecai, Meade, a note from George W.—but I maintain myself in solitude, claiming to be not myself. Who then?

I have been too long out of the life-giving sun. That's my problem.

And I cannot think two thoughts in sequence. *Ahimé.*

June 10

Much better, thank you. Yes, it feels quite good. Now once again I look on the sunny side of defeat.

Facts:

Another call on H.H. Having become accustomed to the plastery whiteness of prisoners and guards alike, the sun-lamped softness of his face (like Tastee White Bread, toasted) seemed more than ever an offense against the natural order. If that is health, then let diseases waste me!

We talked of this, that, and another. He commended my journal's factoricity (sic) in general, but took exception to yesterday's entry, which was too subjective. If I should ever start feeling subjective again, I need only say the word and a guard will bring a tranquilizer. We can't afford to let the precious days slip away from us, can we?

And thus, and so, the greased cams and tappets of his banality bobbed and lolloped up and down, to and fro, upon predictable, rotary paths—and then he asked me: "So you've met Siegfried, have you?"

"Siegfried?" I asked, thinking this might be his nickname for Mordecai.

He winked. "You know . . . Dr. Busk?"

"Siegfried?" I asked once more, more puzzled than before. "How so?"

"You know—like the Siegfried Line. Impregnable. It's because I was sure that she's a cold fish that I had her recruited for this project. Ordinarily it wouldn't do to have women around in a situation like this, having to work with a bunch of horny GIs—and more than one of them colored. But with Siegfried it doesn't make any difference."

"It sounds as if you speak from experience," I suggested.

"WACs" Haast said, shaking his head. "Some of them can't get enough of it. Others . . ." He leaned forward confidentially. "Don't put this into your journal, Sacchetti, but the fact of the matter is that she still has her cherry."

"No!" I protested.

"Don't get me wrong—Siegfried is an A-OK worker. She knows her business like nobody else, and she'd never let her feelings get in the way of business. Psychologists, as a rule, are apt to be sentimental, you know—they like to *help* people. Not Busk. If she has any failing, it's a lack of imagination. Sometimes she's a little limited in her way of thinking. Too . . . you know . . . conventional. Don't misunderstand me—I respect science as much as the next man . . ."

I nodded yes, yes, not misunderstanding him.

"Without science we wouldn't have radiation, or computers, or Krebiozen, or men on the moon. But science is only *one* way of looking at things. Of course I don't let Siegfried say anything directly to the boys"—as Haast calls his guinea pigs—"but I think they can sense her hostility anyhow. Fortunately they haven't let that dampen their enthusiasm. The important thing, as even Busk realizes, is to let them steer their own course. They've got to break away from the old patterns of thought, blaze trails, *explore.*"

"But what is it exactly," I asked, "that Busk doesn't approve of?"

Again he learned forward confidentally, puckering the deltas of tanned wrinkles about his eyes. "There's no reason I shouldn't be the one to tell you, Sacchetti. You'll find out soon enough from one of the boys. Mordecai is going to perform the Magnum Opus!"

"Is he?" I said, savoring Haast's credulity.

He flinched, as sensitive to the first hint of skepticism as a fern to sunlight. "Yes, he is! I know what you're thinking, Sacchetti. You're thinking just what old Siegfried thinks—that Mordecai has me hoodwinked. That I'm being conned, as the saying goes."

"It suggests itself as a possibility," I admitted. Then, salving the wound: "You wouldn't want me to be insincere, would you?"

"No, no—anything but that." He settled back in his chair with a sigh, letting the intently gathered wrinkles

41

diffuse over his face, ripples on the shallow pool of his fatuity.

"I'm not surprised," he went on, "by your attitude. Having read your account of your talk with Mordecai, I should have realized . . . most people have the same reaction at first, you know. They think that alchemy is some kind of black magic. They don't realize it's a *science*, just like any other. The first science, as a matter of fact, and the only science, even now, that isn't afraid to look at *all* the facts. Are you a materialist, Sacchetti?"

"Nooo . . . I wouldn't say that."

"But that's what science has become nowadays! Pure materialism and nothing else. Try and tell somebody about supernatural facts—that is to say, facts that are *superior* to the facts of *natural* science—and they close their eyes and stop their ears. They have no idea of the amount of Study, the hundreds of Volumes, the centuries of Research . . ."

I think he had been about to round out this last phrase with "& Development" but caught himself in time.

"I've noticed," he went on, though veering, "that you mention Thomas Aquinas more than once in your journals. Well, did you ever stop to think that *he* was an alchemist? He was, and his teacher, Albertus Magnus, was an even *greater* alchemist! For centuries the very best minds of Europe studied hermetic science, but nowadays someone like you or Busk comes along and, without bothering to learn a thing about it, you discount all their work as nothing more than just a pack of superstitions. Who's being superstitious though, eh? Who's making judgments without evidence? Eh? Eh? Have you ever read a book about alchemy—one single book?"

I had to admit that I had not read one single book about alchemy.

Haast triumphed: "And yet you think you're qualified to sit in judgment on *centuries* of scholars and dee-vines?" There was an echo in his pronunciation of this word, and indeed in the whole tone and content of his discourse, of Mordecai.

"Take a piece of advice from me, Sacchetti."

"You can call me Louie, sir."

"Yes, that's what I meant to say . . . Louie. Keep an

open mind, and be receptive to Fresh Approaches. All the great advances in Human History, from Galileo"— another splendid, horrendous Mordecaiism—"down through Edison in our own time, have been made by people who dared to be different."

I promised to be open and receptive, but H.H., warmed to his subject, would not abate. He demolished battalions of straw men and demonstrated, with a dreamlike logic, that the whole disheartening story of the last three years in Malaysia has been due to the unreceptivity of certain key figures in Washington, unnamed, to Fresh Approaches.

Whenever I put questions of any particularity to him, however, he grew reticent and canny. I was not ready, he intimated, to be made privy to the mysteries. From his Army days Haast has preserved an unswervable faith in the efficacy of secrets: Knowledge is devalued whenever it becomes too generally known.

I can no longer have any doubt of the fidelity of Berrigan's portrait of "General Uhrlick" in *Mars in Conjunction* (which is not, I've noticed, available at our own library), and I can understand why Haast, though he cried slander to the four winds and did all he could to ruin Berrigan, never dared take him to court. The credulous old fool *did* conduct the whole damned miserable year-long campaign on Auaui by astrology!

Let us hope that history will not repeat itself verbatim, that Mordecai is not, too cunningly, performing Berrigan's fatal role.

Later:

Be it noted: I am reading one single book on alchemy. Haast sent it by messenger within minutes of our leave-taking. Rene Alleau's *Aspects de l'alchemie traditionelle*, with an accompanying typescript translation in a TOP SECRET folder.

It reads, pleasantly enough, like a crank letter, the kind that begins:

Dear Editor,
You probably won't dare to print this letter but . . .

June 11

The *Faustus* rehearsal: a disappointment, a delight, and then the horrid, swift decline to reality.

I don't know what I had been expecting from George W. as a director. Something on the order of the fabeled (and possibly nonexistent) Genet "underground" productions of the late sixties, I suppose. But his design for *Faustus* was a mild pastiche of theater-in-the-round and the laborsome lutulence of Wieland Wagner's stagings for Bayreuth. Of course when the audience consists only of those actors not required onstage—and myself with the promptbook (quite unnecessary as it turned out; even for this first run-through they knew *all* their lines)—a proscenium would be cumbersome and out of keeping. But to suppose that a pea-soup fog is an enhancement to tragedy is mere muddleheadedness, and reactionary to boot. Hell is murky, true—but *Scotland* need not seem so.

So, it appears that (I'm happy to report) our young geniuses can err. This is a judgment, however, based on twenty years of rabid, indiscriminate, and usually disappointed theater-going. The wonder of G.'s *Faustus* is that not he nor any of the prisoners here has ever seen a play on the stage. Movies, yes, and more than once it was by misappropriating camera techniques that G. came a cropper.

But this is all niggling and higgling. As soon as they began to *act*, all the fog rolled back and only admiration was possible. To borrow a phrase from Mordecai: The actors deserve the very highest allocades!

I missed my chance, way back when, to see Burton in the role, but I can't imagine that he would have been much better than George Wagner. Burton's *voice* certainly would have been nobler in that last soliloquy, but could he have convinced one so well that here, in veritas, breathing and whole, was the medieval schoolman, God-haunted

44

and blaspheming God, fatally and heroically in love with Knowledge? Could Burton have made Knowledge seem so horrible and veiled a thing, a succubus, as when, in the opening scene Faustus sighs: "Sweet Analytics, 'tis thou hast ravished me!" When he said that I could feel my arteries dilate to receive, ravished too, her poisons.

Mordecai played Mephistopheles—so much less impressive in Marlowe's than in Goethe's version, though one would not have thought so to see Mordecai tear through it. He delivered the lines that begin "Why this is hell, nor am I out of it" with chilling grace, as though this admission of irrevocable damnation and despair were nothing more than an epigram, some piece of inconsequence by Sheridan or Wilde.

And oh! I might go on praising, singling out a touch here, a phrasing there, a piece of business, but it would come down to the same thing—I would have to relate how in the last act Faustus, lamenting in those last agonized minutes before hell would claim him, suddenly ceased to be Faustus: Again, and with terrible violence, George Wagner lost every scrap and dribble from his stomach. He sobbed and choked, rolling on the slippery stage in a sort of fit, until the guards came to carry him back to the infirmary, leaving the make-believe devils empty-handed in the wings.

"Mordecai," I asked, "what *is* it? Is he still sick? What's wrong with him?"

And Mordecai, icily, not yet out of character: "Why that's the price all good men must pay for knowledge. That's what comes of eating magic apples."

"You mean that the . . . drug they've given you, the drug that's made you so . . . that it can do that too?"

He smiled a pained smile and reached up a heavy hand to remove his horns.

"What the hell," said Murray Sandemann (which—not Something-or-Other—is the surname of the alchemic enthusiast), "why don't you answer asshole's question?"

"Shut up, Murray," Mordecai said.

"Oh, don't worry about me. I won't tell him. It wasn't me, after all, who had him brought here. But now that he is here, isn't it a bit late to be so solicitous of his innocence?"

45

"Just shut up."

"I mean," Murray concluded, "did anyone worry about *our* eating magic apples?"

Mordecai turned to regard me, his dark face almost invisible in the caliginous stagelight. "Do you want your question answered, Sacchetti? Because from now on, if you don't, you shouldn't ask."

"Tell me," I said, feeling trapped into a show of greater daring than I really felt. (Was this how Adam fell?) "I want to know."

"George is dying. He's got a couple weeks left, with any luck. Less, I suppose, after what we've just seen."

"We're *all* dying," Murray Sandemann said.

Mordecai nodded, poker-faced as ever. "We're all dying. From the drug they gave us. Pallidine. It rots the brain. It takes nine months to do the job thoroughly, sometimes a little more, sometimes a little less. And all the while you rot you're getting smarter. Until . . ." Mordecai, his left hand sweeping low, elegantly indicated the pool of George's vomit.

June 12

Up all night—scribble, scribble, scribble. Typically, my reaction to Mordecai's revelation has been to resile, back away, stick my head in the sand—and to write, good God, have I written! With Marlowe's pentameters still reverberating in the murky air, nothing seemed possible but blank verse. Haven't indulged in that since high school. It feels luxurious now, as I run out of fuel, just to type the lines over in stout columns down the page, like caressing fur:

> Ripe as a cage of doves, the rented child,
> With shards of clay pots clinking at each step,
> Stinking of cheap chrism, astride a goat . . .

46

I haven't the least notion what it's all about (the fog is thick) though the title (obscurely) is "The Hierodule." A hierodule, as I discovered last week going through the OED, is a temple slave.

I feel like a goddamned Coleridge, and one whom no visitor from Porlock ever came knocking out of the trance. It began, innocently enough, when I resurrected the aborted "Ceremony" poems of a year ago, but the only connection with those pious trifles is the opening image of the priest entering the temple-labyrinth:

> . . . Turning left, turning right, gasping at eyes
> Lovely as a god's. The blood flutters into the pool . . .

Then, within ten lines it degenerates (or ascends?) into something that wholly defies my powers of synopsis, much less analysis. Pagan it is, most certainly, and perhaps heretical as well. I would never dare let it be published under my own name. Published! I'm too giddy yet to know if the damned thing scans, much less whether it's publishable.

But I have the feeling, which comes after a good poem, that everything else I've ever done *is* dross in comparison. This, for instance—the description of the idol:

> Behold! behold the black, ungrainèd flesh,
> The jaw's jeweled hinge that we can barely glimpse . . .

> . . .

> While, within, the poison'd hierodule,
> Dying, whispers what the god had meant. . . .

I wish he'd whisper it to me though.
110 lines!
I feel as though a week has gone by since I sat down yesterday afternoon to start to work at it.

June 13

George Wagner is dead. The sealed casket, freighted with what scraps of flesh the clinic has no use for, was fitted into a slot crudely dug into the native rock of this place, our very own mausoleum. Myself, the other prisoners, and three guards attended, but neither Haast nor Busk nor yet any chaplain. Were there chaplains at Ravensbruck, do you suppose? To my own and the general embarrassment, I mouthed some hollow prayers, sad as lead. Unascended, I imagine they are lying still on the rough floor of the crypt.

The hypogeum, half lit, with its twenty-odd unfilled niches, possessed for the prisoners (like the rows of coffin-beds in a Carthusian monastery) the inexpungeable fascination of a memento mori. It was this morbid impulse, I suspect, rather than any pious feeling for the dead, that had brought them to the inhumation.

As the others filed out the door into the geometric calm of our corridor world, Mordecai laid a hand upon the stone wall (not chill, as one expects of stone, but warm as living flesh) and said, "Breccia." I had thought he had been going to say, "Good-bye."

"Let's get a move on," one of the guards said. I've been here long enough now that I can sort out the faces and persons of the guards; this was Rock-Eye. His fellows were Fartpuff and Assiduous.

Mordecai stooped to pick off the floor a fist-sized chunk of stone. Assiduous removed his side arm from its holster. Mordecai laughed. "I'm not inciting to riot, Mister Patrolman, honest I'm not. I'd just like this pretty piece of breccia for my rock collection." He pocketed it.

"Mordecai," I said. "About what you told me after the rehearsal . . . how long will it be before you . . . how long, do you expect to. . . ?"

48

Mordecai, standing already at the threshold, turned, silhouetted by the fluorescence of the corridor. "I'm in my seventh month now," he said evenly. "Seven months and ten days. Which gives me another fifty days—unless I'm premature." He stepped down from the sill of the door and turned to the left, out of sight.

"Mordecai," I said, starting after him.

Rock-Eye blocked my path. "Not just now, Mr. Sacchetti, if you please. You have an appointment to see Dr. Busk." Fartpuff and Assiduous stepped into position on either side of me. "If you'll just follow me?"

"It was a very foolish, a very unwise, and a very injudicious thing to do," Dr. Aimée Busk repeated in grave, guidance-counselor tones. "Oh, not the matter of asking after poor young George—because, as you point out, we wouldn't have been able to keep that aspect of the situation hidden from you much longer in any case. We had been hoping, you see, to discover an . . . antidote. But we find that the process, once begun, is irreversible. Alas. No, it is not *that* that I was speaking of, because for all you may protest about what you choose to call our inhumanity, there is ample precedent for what we're about. Throughout its history, medical research has paid for its progress with the blood of martyrs."

She paused, pleased with the resonance.

"What is it then, if not that, that you called me in here to be scolded for?"

"For that very foolish, very unwise, very injudicious little research expedition in the library."

"You keep a sharp lookout."

"Well, of course. Will you excuse me if I smoke? Thank you." She fitted a crumbling Camel into a stubby, plastic cigarette holder, once transparent, now stained to the same deep brown as her middle and forefinger.

"But whether I looked into *Who's Who* now or after I was released, you'll have to admit that the information is easily come by."

What I had found in *Who's Who* (there is no reason why I shouldn't mention it *now*) has been the identity of the corporation that employs Haast as vice-president in charge of Research &

49

THOMAS M. DISCH

[Here two lines have been defaced from the manuscript of Louis Sacchetti's journal. Ed.]

"Bad faith? Deception?" Dr. Busk said, gently remonstrating. "If there's been any deception, then you've certainly been as much a party to it as I. But isn't it really more a question of morale? We've just been trying to keep you cheered up, so that your work needn't be hampered with needless anxietization."

"So in fact from the first you've never had any intention of releasing me from Camp Archimedes?"

"Never? Oh, now you're dramatizing. Of course we'll let you out. Sometime or other. When the climate of opinion is right. When the experiment has justified itself to our PR department. *Then* we can return you to Springfield. And since we'll almost certainly reach that point within the next five years—within as many months, more likely— you should be grateful for the opportunity to spend that time here, in the very van of progress, rather than there, where you were so bored."

"Yes, I really ought to thank you for the chance to witness all your murders. Yes indeed."

"Well, of course . . . if that's how you *will* regard it. But you should know by now, Mr. Sacchetti, that the world sees things differently than you do. If you should try to make a scandal about Camp Archimedes, you'll probably find yourself as little heeded as you were little heeded at your trial. Oh, you'll find a few fellow paranoids to listen to your brave speeches, but on the whole people just won't take conchies seriously, you know."

"On the whole, people don't take their consciences seriously."

"A different hypothesis, but it fits the same set of facts, doesn't it?" Dr. Busk raised a minuscule, ironic eyebrow, and then (as though that had been the necessary bootstrap) herself from the low leather seat. Her crisp gray dress, smoothed by her nervous hands, whispered electrically. "Is there anything else, Mr. Sacchetti?"

"You had said, when the subject first arose, that you would explain more fully the action of this drug, this Pallidine."

"So I did, so I shall." She sat back down in the web of

50

black leather, groomed her pale lips into a teacherly smile, and exposited:

"The causative agent of the disease—though is it fair, actually, to call it a disease, when it does so much good? —is a little bug, a spirochete, nearly related to the *Treponema pallidum*. You've heard it referred to as 'Pallidine' here, a name that rather glosses over the fact that the agent infecting the host is, unlike most pharmaceuticals, living, self-reproducing. In short, a bug.

"Perhaps you've heard tell of the *Treponema pallidum?* Or, as it may also be called, the *Spirochaetae pallida?* No? Well, you'd know it well enough by its fruits. *Treponema pallidum* is the initiator of syphilis. Ah, there's the old shock of recognition, eh!

"The particular bug we have to deal with here is something of a sport, a latter-day offshoot of a subgroup known as the Nicols variety, which was isolated in 1912 from the infected brain of a syphilitic man and kept alive thereafter in the bloodstreams of bunny rabbits. Countless generations of Nicols treponemes spawned themselves in those laboratory rabbits, and always they were accorded the most intensive investigation—one might almost say reverence. Especially since 1949. In '49 Nelson and Mayer, two fellow Americans, developed the T.P.I., the single finest diagnostic test for the disease. All this, by the by. The treponeme that has done in young George is at least as different from the Nicols treponeme as that is from your garden-variety *Treponema pallidum*.

"It shouldn't astonish you to learn that by far the most active researcher into the little world of the spirochete has been the Armed Services. Many a good fighting man has been defeated by that microscopic enemy, until, of course, the Second World War and the advent of penicillin. Even then, research was not abandoned. About five years ago an Army team was investigating—on rabbits, naturally—the possible utility of radiation as a therapeutic tool in cases where the usual penicillin treatment can't be used, or when—about three percent of the time—it doesn't take. A curious situation was observed—the experiment seemed to have produced a new bloodline of rabbits. A bloodline, that is to say, not in the reproductive sense, but rather the succession of rabbits who receive blood—

and treponemes—from each other. One particular line of rabbits developed not only the typical orchitis, but they seemed to have become, despite the ravages of the disease, quite *shrewd*. Several times they escaped from their cages. Their performances in Skinner boxes surpassed anything that had ever been recorded. I was in charge of their testing, and I can assure you it was a *most* astonishing achievement. Well that, of course, was the discovery of Pallidine. Three more years were to go by before anything was to be made of that discovery. Three years!

"Under the microscope, Pallidine looks much the same as any other spirochete. It is, as the name suggests, spiral in shape, with seven coils. The average *Treponema pallidum* is much larger, though it may have as few as six coils in rare instances. If you'd like to see one, I'm sure . . . No? They're really rather pretty. They propel themselves by stretching out lengthwise, concertina-fashion, then contracting. Very graceful. 'Sylphlike' is what the textbooks call it. I've spent entire hours just watching them swim about in plasma.

"Oh, there are a host of differences between *Treponema pallidum* and Pallidine, but what it is *exactly* that gives the latter its special potency we've not been able to determine. Syphilis in its late stages is notorious for its attacks on the central nervous system. For instance, when the spirochetes have worked their way into the spinal cord—and this may be quite twenty years after the initial infection—you get tabes dorsalis—that's the most common effect, and very nasty. You don't know tabes? Well, it's true that nowadays one sees less of it. It starts out by just making the legs wobble, then the joints swell and melt until they can afford no support whatever, and finally about ten percent of those who get it go blind. That's tabes, but when the spirochetes get to the brain— they work their way up the spinal cord osmotically, rather the way sap rises in a tree—that's when you get general paresis, which has a much more interesting pathology. Several well-known cases would appeal to you, as an artist—Donizetti, Gauguin, and, not least, the philosopher Nietzsche, who signed his last letters from the asylum 'Dionysius.' "

"No poets of note?" I asked.

"As a matter of fact, the disease takes its name from a poet, Fracastorius, who wrote a pastoral in 1530, in Latin verse, about the shepherd Syphilis, a lovesick swain. I've never read it myself, but if you'd like . . . ? Then, too, there are the Goncourts, Abbé Galiani, Hugo Wolff . . . but the supreme and undying example of what the *Treponema pallidum* can accomplish is Adolph Hitler.

"Now, if the spirochete accomplished nothing more in the brain than this sort of havoc—deliriums and disintegration—Camp Archimedes would not exist. But it has been suggested—and by some very reputable people, though they were not usually in the medical line—that neuro-syphilis is as often beneficent as it is at other times malign, that the geniuses I've mentioned, and many others that I might add, were as much its beneficiaries as its victims.

"It is all a question, finally, of the nature of genius. The best explanation of genius that I know, the one that incorporates most of the facts we have, is Koestler's—that the act of genius is simply the bringing together of two hitherto distinct spheres of reference, or matrices—a talent for juxtapositions. Archimedes' bath is a small instance. Till him no one had associated measurements of mass with the commonplace observation of water displacement. The question is, for a modern investigator, what actually takes place *in the brain* at the moment that an Archimedes says, 'Eureka!' It seems clear, now, that it is a sort of breakdown—literally, the mind disintegrates, and the old, distinct categories are for a little while fluid and capable of re-formation."

"But it's just that," I objected, "the re-formation of the disrupted categories, in which the act of genius consists. It's not the breakdown that counts, but the new juxtapositions that follow. Madmen can break down just as spectacularly as geniuses."

Dr. Busk smiled, enigmatic in her veil of cigarette smoke. "Perhaps that thin line that is said to separate genius from madness is only fortuitous. Perhaps the madman simply has the bad luck of being wrong. But your point is taken, and I can reply to it. You would suggest, I take it, that genius is only one per cent inspiration, that the process of preparing for the moment when the 'Eureka!' comes is

53

what is crucial in the formation of genius. In short, his education, by which he becomes acquainted with reality.

"But doesn't that just beg the question? Education, memory itself, is but the recapitulation of all the moments of genius in that culture. Education is always breaking down old categories and recombining them in better ways. And who has a better memory, strictly speaking, than the catatonic who resurrects some part of the past in all its completeness, annihilating the present moment utterly? I might go so far as to say that thought itself is a disease of the brain, a degenerative condition of matter.

"Why, if genius were a *continuous* process, instead of what it is—a fluke—it would be of no value to us whatsoever! Geniuses in a field like mathematics are usually played out by thirty, at the very latest. The mind defends itself against the disintegrative process of creativity. It begins to jell, notions solidify into inalterable *systems,* which simply refuse to be broken down and re-formed. Consider Owens, the great anatomist of the Victorian age, who simply *wouldn't* understand Darwin. It's self-preservation, pure and simple.

"And then think of what happens if genius *doesn't* rein itself in but insists on plunging on ahead into the chaos of freest association. I'm thinking of that hero of you literateurs, James Joyce. I know any number of psychiatrists who could, in good conscience, have accepted *Finnegan Wakes* [sic] as the very imprimatur of madness and had its author hospitalized on its evidence alone. A genius? Oh yes. But all we common people have the common sense to realize that genius, like the clap, is a social disease, and we take action accordingly. We put all our geniuses in one kind or another of isolation ward, to escape being infected.

"If you need any further proof of what I'm saying then look about you. We have geniuses on every hand here, and what is their chief concern? To what noble purpose do they apply the vast stock of their combined intelligences? To the study of chimeras! To alchemy!

"Oh, I'm sure that no one, not Dr. Faustus himself, has ever applied a keener intelligence, a finer discernment, or a profounder awareness to the hermetic arts. As Mordecai is always ready to point out, centuries of the cleverist riddlemakers and the sliest obscurantists have busied themselves elaborating these intellectual arabesques. It is quite *deep* enough for the tallest mind to drown in. But for all that, it's a pack of nonsense, as you and I and Mordecai Washington perfectly well know."

"Haast doesn't seem to think so," I said mildly.

"As we also are well aware, Haast is a damned fool," Busk said, stubbing out her Camel, which she had smoked down to the plastic holder.

"Oh, I wouldn't say that," I said.

"Because he reads your journal—as I do. You can't very well deny what you've already written there. You've said what you think of Mordecai's ideas and the way he's snowing Haast."

"Perhaps, I've a broader mind than you'd like to give me credit for. I'll reserve my judgment on Mordecai's theories, if it's all the same to you."

"You're a bigger hypocrite than I'd thought, Sacchetti. Believe any nonsense you like, and tell whatever lies you have a mind to. It makes no difference to me. I'll have my showdown with that charlatan soon enough."

"How so?" I asked.

"It's all scheduled. I'll see you have a ringside ticket for the main event."

"When is it to be?"

"Why, on Midsummer's Eve. When else?"

Later:
A handwritten note from Haast: Good for you, Louie! Stick up for your rights! We'll show that smart-assed bitch a thing or two next week. You'd better believe it!

All the best,
H.H.

June 15

This is your old friend Louie too (or, popularly, Louis the Likewise) with wonderful new news for all you sufferers from angst and angina, for the conscience-ridden and God-plagued, for the psychosomatic and the simply stigmatic. You can throw away that truss! Because, mon semblable, mon frère, there is nothing but an aching emptiness at the center of things, alleluia! And not even aching any more, no, the void is happy as the day is long. *That* is the secret that those ancients possessed, that is the truth that will make us free, you and me. Say it three times in the morning and three times, at night: There is no God, there never was, and never will be, world without end, amen.

Would you deny it, old Adamite, Louie I? Then let me recommend you to your own poem, the poem you claimed not to be able to understand. *I* understand it: The idol is empty; his speech an imposture. There is no Baal, my friend, only the whisperer within, putting your words in His mouth. A farrago of anthropomorphism. Deny it! Not all your piety nor wit, my boy!

And O! O! those precious, fawning poems of yours, licking the golden ass of your let's-pretend God-daddy. What shit, eh? Years and years of it, piling it on, like the birdy (Augustine's, isn't it?) that tried to move a mountain, a pebble at a time, each time a chilead, and when the last granule had been translated not an eyeblink of eternity had gone by. But *you,* sparrowfart, didn't even attack mountains. The *Hills* of Switzerland—and then, for a sequel? The Turds of the Vatican?

Ha, I hear, as from a great distance, your mild protest: The fool says in his heart there is no God.

And the wise man says it aloud.

Later, much later:
I need not explain, I think, that I've been feeling poorly

today and yesterday. I have remarked already in this journal, I think, that I had thought Dr. Mieris had cured me of my megrims. I had also thought he'd cured me of such scherzoes as the above represents.

Think.

Thought.

Thunk.

The ground is still quaggy, and though I am myself again, it doesn't feel quite permanent, this self-possession. I am sackless, wearied by *his* excesses, and my head hurts; it is late.

I have been walking the corridors, corridors, corridors. Considering what Busk had to say, until I was forced to consider the graver matters brought forward by Louie II. To him I make no reply, as that devil is as good a theologian as I, tautologically.

Silence, then. But isn't silence tantamount, almost, to admitting defeat? Alone and unhoused, I lack grace: That is all that is the matter.

O God, simplify these equations!

June 16

"Morituri te salutamus," Mordecai said, opening the door, grinning, to which I, all lackluster, had no better reply than a thumbs-up sign.

"Quid nunc?" he asked, closing the door—a question I felt even less competent to answer. Indeed, the whole purpose of my visit was to avoid confronting myself with the problem of What-now.

"Charity," I replied. "What other reason would I have for lightening your gloomy cell?" A fey touch, which, falling flat, only heaped on more gloom.

"A base of charity," Mordecai said, "neutralizes the acids of self-doubt."

"Do you get copies of my journal too?" I asked.

"No, but I see a lot of Haast, and we worry about you.

You wouldn't write something in your journal, you know, that you really wanted to keep a secret, so there's no reason to make faces. Your problem, Sacchetti, is intellectual pride. You like to make a fucking song and dance out of every spiritual itch and tremble you get. Now, what I'd suggest, if you're going to lose your faith is that you goddam well go to a dentist and have it *pulled*. It hurts only if you keep playing with it."

"But I came here to interest myself in *your* problems, Mordecai. I want just to forget my own."

"Yes, yes. Well then, make yourself at home. I've enough problems for both of us." He whistled shrilly and called: "Opsi! Mopsi! Cottontail! Come and shake hands with your new little brother." He turned back to address me: "May I present my three familiars? My fire-drakes?"

Out of the sweltering darkness of the room (lighted only by two candles on a table against the far wall, and a third that M. held in his hand) three rabbits came hopping forward cautiously. One was an unblemished white, the other two piebald.

"Opsi," Mordecai said. "Shake hands with my friend Donovan."

I crouched low, and the white rabbit hopped two hops closer, sniffed perspicaciously, raised itself on its hind feet, and extended its right forepaw, which I took between thumb and forefinger to shake.

"How do you do, Opsi," I said.

Opsi withdrew his furry paw from my grasp and backed off.

"Opsi?" I asked Mordecai.

"Short for opsimath—one who begins to learn late in life. We're all opsimaths here. Now Mopsi, it's your turn."

The second rabbit, speckled brown and black, advanced. When it had reared itself on its hind legs I could see what appeared to be udders on its underbelly, though of quite disproportionate size. I pointed these out to M.

"It's the orchitis, you know—inflammation of the testicles. That's the price *they* pay for being so bright."

I let go Mopsi's paw abruptly, startling all three rabbits back to their hidlings in the dark room.

"Oh, don't worry about germs. Only if you were to put that finger in your mouth . . . spirochetes need a warm, damp place to grow. That's what makes venereal disease so venereal. You can disinfect yourself in my can, but first, can't I call Cottontail back? He must be feeling quite insecure, the way you've scanted him."

Reluctantly I shook hands with Cottontail. Afterward I washed with soap and cold water.

"Where's Peter?" I asked, lathering a second time.

"Farmer MacGregor got to him," Mordecai answered from the obscurity. "The rabbits don't last as long as we do. Two, three weeks, and then, Phut!"

Returning to the larger room from the fluorescent bath, I was temporarily blinded. "You should try gaslight, Mordecai. A wonderful invention of this modern age."

"In fact I *have* gaslight on days when my eyes aren't on the blink. But days like today a bright light would go through my tender jellies like a hail of needles. Shall I tell you about my other diseases? Will you commiserate?"

"If it would be any comfort to you."

"Oh, an Egyptian comfort. For the first two months there was nothing that seems particularly memorable *now* —a few gumboils, a rash, swellings—nothing that any practiced hypochondriac couldn't do for himself. Then, in the third month, I came down with laryngitis, concurrently with an overriding enthusiasm for mathematics. A convenient hobby for mutes, eh? Soon afterward my liver started to decay and the whites of my eyes turned yellow. Ever since I've been living on mashed potatoes, boiled fruit, fancy desserts, and all that kind of puke. No meat, no fish, no liquor. Not that I very much want liquor. I mean, I don't need more mental stimulation than I've got, do I? During the hepatitis was when I had my first big literary kick and learned French and German—and when I wrote that story that I still haven't shown you. Don't leave this room without you take that story with you— you hear, Sacchetti?"

"I'd already intended to ask you for it."

"By the fourth month I was just one bundle of ills. The difficulty in describing them is that in a retrospective narration I give my diseases too crisp edges. In the event, phases blurred and overlapped. Gumboils and rashes didn't stop just because something else started, and there've been obscure cramps and sudden squitters and jactitations that

59

came and left in a day or an hour. With all the symptoms I've had at one time or another, I've just about exhausted *Hasting's Encyclopaedia of Pathology.*"

"*Of Religion and Ethics,* isn't it?"

"I've exhausted that too."

"But *when?* When have you fitted in all this education? That's what I can't understand. Where did you find the time, in seven months, to pick up . . . everything?"

"Sit down, Sacchetti, and I'll tell you all about it. But do me a favor first—bring me that thermos on my desk. That's a good sport."

My eyes had adjusted to the half light of the room, and I could make my way to the table unstumbling. A sweating thermos lay upon a TOP SECRET file folder of the sort Haast had sent to me. It's wet base had made a ring stain on the stiff paper.

"Thanks," Mordecai said, taking the thermos and uncorking it. He was half reclined on a low divan of striped silk, propped up with a ratchel of small soft cushions. One of the piebald rabbits had come to cuddle in his crotch.

He drank from the thermos noisily. "I'd offer you some, but . . ."

"Thanks just the same. I'm not thirsty."

"The question, you see, isn't how do I do it, but how do I *stop* doing it. I don't stop doing it, and that's half my misery. In my worst moments, with my head in the pisser, retching, the old brainjelly goes right on fermenting, oblivious to the low soma. No, not oblivious, just indifferent, aloof, a spectator. I become more intrigued with the fauve colors of my heavings or the chemistry of stomach acids than with the merely local miseries of my guts. I'm always thinking, speculating, figuring. It never stops, that brainjelly, just as the heart or the lungs don't stop. Even sitting here talking, my mind is flying off on tangents, into vortices, trying to tie all the loose ends of the universe into a single knot of consciousness. It doesn't fucking stop. At night I need injections before I can sleep, and asleep I dream technicolor nightmares of exemplary and, as far as I know, wholly original terror. Quite cud-blurbling. That's a spoonerism, somewhat."

"Yes, I noticed."

"One thing, though—one thing *will* stop it for a little

while—when I have a stroke. Then I am happily blank for an hour after."

"You have strokes too."

"At closer intervals. They are the labor pains with which I prepare to deliver my spirit to the void. Aortitis—that's the latest inside story. My aorta is de-elasticized, and now, I understand, the valve is going. Blood leaks back into the left ventricle at every stroke, and the old ticker, as we fondly call it, speeds up to compensate. But soon enough—Phut! One more little rabbit lost in the lists of science." He laid two heavy black hands upon the nestling rabbit and closed his eyes. "Isn't it pathetic?"

Without rising from the hassock, I occupied the time (become suddenly vacant, like a punctured Gemini capsule that loses its air in one quick *Whuppf!*) with a silent survey of Mordecai's room. Only as large as mine, its enfouldered darkness created an illusion of indefinite spaciousness, out of which arose, intermittently, the hypotheses of furniture. Faustian bookshelves rose to the ceiling on all the walls except where the divan stood, above which hung a copy of the Ghent altarpiece, its disparities from the original masked by the benign obscurity.

Near the overburdened worktable (which occupied almost the whole of what in the arrangement of my room was the sleeping ell) was a mechanical apparatus or stabile sculpture, some four feet high, that consisted of several upthrusting rods tipped with small metallic balls that glinted in the candlelight, surrounding a central, larger globe, goldenly gleaming—all these elements bounded in an imaginary sphere defined by two thick circumscriptive bands of iron.

"That?" Mordecai said. "That's my orrery. Built to my own specifications. The several motions of each little moon and planet are regulated by sub-sub-sub-to-the-nth-miniaturized radio elements within. Straight from the pages of *Popular Electronics,* isn't it?"

"But what is it *for?*"

"It holds the mirror up to nature—isn't that enough? I did dabble in astrology once upon a time, but even then it had no more than symbolic significance. For the real work there's an observatory upstairs. Ah, did your eyes light up

61

with speculations then? Glimmerings of a great escape? Forget it, Sacchetti. We never get beyond a little planetarium, to which the telescope's images are broadcast by closed-circuit TV.".

"You say 'once upon a time.' Does that mean you've given astrology up?"

Mordecai sighed. "Life is so short. There isn't room for everything. Think of all the broads I'll never lay now, the songs I'll never dance to. And I would have liked a chance to go to Europe too and have a quick look-see at all the things I've been reading about. Culture. But it wasn't in my stars. I'll always envy you that trip to Europe. All the places I'd like to go. Rome, Florence, Venice. English cathedrals. Mont-Saint-Michel. The Escorial. Bruges and"—with a gesture to the gilt-framed picture of the bleeding lamb—"Ghent. Everywhere, in fact, but where you *did* go, you dumb bastard. Switzerland and Germany! Jesus Christ, what were you fucking around *there* for? I mean, what are mountains? They're warts on the face of the earth. And as for anything *north* of the Alps . . . well, I was stationed four years just outside Heidelberg, and as far as I'm concerned Europe stops at the Rhine. The best proof of which is the fact that I enjoyed every beer-swilling, dumpling-sodden minute of my leaves. Except when the locals stared too much at my to-them-amazing pigmentation and I got to feeling like a leftover from Buchenwald. Deutschland!" Mordecai concluded his commination with such vehemence that the rabbit scampered from his lap in terror. "I'd as soon take a vacation in Mississippi."

This led to a few reminiscences on my part of my Fulbright year, pleasant enough to recount but beside the point here, together with a guilty *précis* of my reasons (literary, musical) for having quit Europe for Germany (a distinction I tacitly acknowledged).

"Rilke, Schmilke!" Mordecai said when I'd finished. "You can read *books* here. Admit it—the fascination of Germany in this century is the fascination of the abomination. You go there to catch a whiff of the smoke that still hangs in the air. Tell me one thing—did you make a side trip to Dachau, or didn't you?"

I had, and told him. He wanted me to describe the

town and the camp, and I complied. His appetite for detail was greater than my memory could satisfy, though I surprised myself with the circumstantiality I was able to muster: It had been a long while since I'd been there.

"I only asked," Mordecai said, when he was convinced the wells of memory were dry, "because I've been dreaming about deathcamps lately. An understandable preoccupation, wouldn't you say? Admittedly, it's only an analogy to our little home in the west here. Except that I'm a prisoner and except that I'm marked for extermination, *I* can't complain. And isn't everybody, after all?"

"A prisoner? I often get that feeling—yes."

"No, I meant marked for slaughter. The difference is I've had the bad luck to sneak a look at the execution orders, while most people walk off to the ovens thinking they're going to take a shower." He laughed harshly, turning sideways on the divan, to see me better, as I now stood on the other side of the room, by the clockwork of the orrery.

"It isn't just Germany," he said. "And it isn't just Camp Archimedes. It's the whole universe. The whole goddamned universe is a fucking concentration camp."

Mordecai rolled back into the pile of tasseled cushions, coughing and laughing at once, knocking the half-filled thermos over on the Persian carpet that covered the tiled floor. He caught it up, found it empty, and with a curse flung it across the room, rupturing a panel of the painted screen partitioning one corner of the room.

"Push the button beside the door, will you, Sacchetti? I need some more of the sickening sugarwater they call coffee here. That's a good sport."

Almost immediately I'd rung, a black-uniformed guard (Fartpuff it was) arrived with a coffee wagon laden with pastries, from which Mordecai made selections. To me another attendant handed three Spode bowls filled with fresh carrot slices.

Mordecai pushed back the detritus of books and papers from the edge of his worktable, making room for our saucers and the tray of pastries. He bit into a large chocolate eclair, squirting whipped cream from the other end onto a sheet of typed numbers.

"I keep wishing," he said, his mouth full, "that it were meat."

The rabbits meanwhile had climbed atop the desk and were nibbling their carrots discreetly. Even in candlelight I could see the distinct spoor of quittors that they had trailed across the open books and SECRET file folders.

"Feel free, feel free," Mordecai said, helping himself to a piece of cheesecake.

"Thank you, but really I'm not hungry."

"Don't mind me than. I am."

I did my best not to mind him, but to do so it was necessary to turn my attention elsewhere, and so for the space of two cups of coffee and four large pastries I was able to do a random sampling of the uppermost deposits on Mordecai's worktable. The following inventory needs must omit all that lay outside the three circles of candlelight, as well as whatever earlier Troys of thought were buried below.

I saw:

Several books on alchemy—the *Tabula smargdina*, Benedictus Figulus' *A golden and blessed casket of Nature's marvels*, Gerber's *Works*, Poisson's *Nicolas Flamel*, etc.—many in the last stages of picturesqueness;

Tables of random numbers;

Three or four electronics texts—the largest, *DNA Engineering* by California Tech's Wunderkind Kurt Vreden, in typescript with an enticing CONFIDENTIAL label pasted to the cardboard binder;

Several color plates torn from Skira art books, chiefly of works of the Flemish masters, though there was a detail from Raphael's *School of Athens* and a tattered print of Dürer's woodcut *Melancholia*;

A plastic skull, very decorative, with paste-glass ruby eyes;

Enid Starkie's biography of Rimbaud, and Pléiade edition of the poet's works;

Volume IV of *Hasting's Encyclopaedia*, onto the open pages of which Mordecai (or one of the rabbits?) had overturned an ink bottle;

Wittgenstein's *Tractatus Logico-Philosophicus*, with some of the same ink on its leather binding (I recall now,

64

as I make this inventory, what use Luther made of ink-pots);

Yarrowsticks;

Several file folders, of various colors—orange, tan, gray, black—their typed labels seldom legible in the poor light, except the nearest, *Expense Book* by G. Wagner. From the pages of this (whether proper to it and falling out or only a bookmark, I cannot say) projected a crackly vellum sheet with a crude drawing on it, in colored inks, not much superior to an average men's room graffito. That part of the drawing I could see represented a crowned and bearded man holding a tall scepter upon which were mounted, one above the other, six further crowns. The king stood upon an odd pedestal that grew flowerlike from a vine that branched, above the kings head, into a sort of lattice. At the interstices of this lattice were six other male heads, lower, lesser types, and beside each head a letter of the alphabet, from *D* through *I*. The left-hand portion of this head-bearing vine curled out of sight into George's closed book;

And, covering all else, heaps of Mordecai's shorthand scribblings, among which were several drawings even more crudely rendered than the one I've just described.

End of inventory.

Except for occasional abstracted endearments to the rabbits (which, finished with their own snack, sniffed at the pastry plate), Mordecai was quiet while he gorged on the pastries. After a final strawberry tart, however, he became talkative again, not to say manic:

"Is it hot enough for you? I really ought to turn down the oven when company comes, but then I get the shivers. Would you like to see a genuine philosophical egg? No alchemist can be without one. Of course you would. Come —I'll unveil all the mysteries for you today."

I followed him to the farther, screened corner of the room and noticed how, as we approached, the heat increased. By the squat, tiled furnace that the screen had concealed, the air was heated to sauna temperatures.

"Lo!" Mordecai intoned. "The athanor!"

From a shelf on the wall he took down two heavy face shields, handing one to me. "These are for when the nuptial chamber is opened," he explained, poker-faced.

65

"You'll have to excuse my athanor. It's electric, which isn't quite *comme il faut*"—pronounced by Mordecai, come-ill-phut—"I'll admit, but it's much easier this way to maintain a fire that is vaporous, digesting, continuous, nonviolent, subtle, encompassed, airy, obstructive, and corrupting. We pursue the traditional ends of alchemy here, but I've taken a few liberties with some of the means we employ.

"Now, if you'll put on that mask, I can let you peek into mother's belly, as it's fondly known in the trade."

The mask's eyeslits were shielded with tinted glass. Putting it on in the dark room I was, effectually, blinded.

"Ecce," Mordecai said, and the top of the tiled furnace slid aside with a mechanical whirr, exposing the glowing concavity, within which stood a darkly gleaming, oblate object about two feet high—the philosophical egg (or, prosaically, a retort). It was about as interesting as a Dutch oven, which it somewhat resembled.

The lid hummed shut, and I slipped the sweat-wet mask from my face.

"A log fire *would* have been more spooky," I said.

"The end justifies the means. This is going to *work*."

"Mmm," I said, returning to my hassock on the other side of the room, where it was a moderate ninety degrees.

"It *will* work," he insisted, following.

"What exactly are you cooking in your big pot? Transmuting a base metal to gold? Poetic associations apart, what's the use? There are many elements these days rarer than gold. Hasn't it become a rather quixotic ambition in this post-Keynesian age?"

"I made that very point to Haast some months ago, when the experiment was being designed. Accordingly, the metallic opus is only a step on our way, the ultimate goal being the distillation of an elixir for our joint benefit." Mordecai smiled. "An elixir of long life."

"Of youth, I'd thought it was called."

"That, of course, is its fascination for Haast."

"And how is this potion being brewed? I suppose your recipe is a close-kept secret."

"In some particulars, yes, though it can be rooted out from Geber and Paracelsus. But really, Sacchetti, would you *want* to know? Would you risk salvation to find out?

Would you want me to risk mine? Raymond Lully says, 'I swear to you upon my soul that if you reveal this, you shall be damned.' Of course, if you'll be content with an inspecific account . . ."

"Whatever Isis is willing to unveil."

"The philosophical egg—the big pot that you saw in the athanor—contains an electuary dissolved in water, which for the past ninety-four days has been exposed alternately to the heat of telluric fires during the day, and at night to the light of the star Sirius. Properly speaking, gold is not a metal, it is light. Sirius has always been thought especially efficacious in operations of this sort, but in past ages it was difficult to capture the Sirian light in a pure state, as the light from neighboring stars was apt to adulterate it, minorating its special properties. Here a radio telescope is employed to ensure the necessary homogeneity. Did you see the lens sealed into the top of the egg? That focuses the pure beam upon the bride and groom within, sulphur and mercury."

"I thought you were after Sirian light. You're getting radio waves."

"So much the better. It's only human frailty that draws a distinction between radio and light waves. If we were only spiritual enough, we'd see the radio waves too. But to return—in nine and ninety days, on the Eve of Midsummer, the sepulcher will be opened, and the elixir decanted. But you shouldn't laugh, you know. It spoils the whole effect."

"I'm sorry. I try not to, but you're really so expert at this. I keep thinking of Ben Jonson."

"You think I'm not serious."

"Terrifically serious. And the stage effects are better than anything George came up with for *Doctor Faustus*—those jars of fetuses in the bookcase, that chalice . . . it's consecrated, of course?"

Mordecai nodded.

"I knew it. And those rings you're wearing today—Masonic rings?"

"Of great antiquity." He wiggled his fingers proudly.

"You put on a grandstand show, Mordecai, but what will you do for an encore?"

"If it doesn't come off this time, I don't have to worry

about encores, you know. The deadline nighs. But it *will* work, goddamn it! I'm not even worried about that."

I shook my head, perplexed. I could not decide if Mordecai had taken himself in with his own splendid charlatanry or if these credos were just a necessary adjunct to the larger deception, a sideshow, as it were. I even began to wonder if, given enough time, he couldn't convert me to his folly—if not by means of reasoned argument then simply by the sublime example of his deadpan and unremitting earnestness.

"Why does it seem so ridiculous to you?" Mordecai asked, deadpan, unremitting, earnest.

"It's the combination of fancy and fact, of madness and analysis. Those books on your desk, for example—the Wittgenstein and the Vreden. You do really read them, don't you?" He nodded. "And I believe you do. That, and then beside it, the sheer chicanery of Byronic diabolism, the silliness of cooking pots and bottled fetuses."

"Well, I do what I can to bring alchemic procedures up to date, but my attitude to pure Science, capital S, was stated a century ago by a fellow alchemist, Arthur Rimbaud—*Science est trop lente*. It's too slow. How much more so for me than him! How much time is left me? A month, two. And if I had years instead of months, what difference would that make? Science acquiesces, fatally, to the second law of thermodynamics—magic is free to be a conscientious objector. The fact is that I'm not *interested* in a universe in which I have to die."

"Which is to say that you've chosen self-delusion."

"Indeed, no! I choose to escape. I choose freedom."

"You've come to a splendid place to find it."

Mordecai, growing ever more restless, rolled off the divan, where he had only just reclined, and began to pace the room, gesticulating. "Why, this is *exactly* where my freedom is largest. The best we can hope for, in a finite and imperfect world, is that our minds be free, and Camp Archimedes is uniquely equipped to allow me just that freedom and no other. Perhaps I might make an exception for the Institute for Advanced Studies at Princeton, as well, since, as I understand it, it's organized along very much the same lines. Here, you see, I can hold everything in despite. Anywhere else one begins tactily to accept one's circumstances, one ceases to struggle, to engage each new wrong and ugliness in combat, one becomes hopelessly compromised."

"Nonsense and sophistry. You're just trying on theories for size."

"Ah, you see into my very soul, Sacchetti. But there is, after all, a point to my nonsense and sophistry. Make your Catholic Gaud the warden of this prison-universe, and you have exactly Aquinas' argument, nonsensical, sophistical—that it is only in submitting to His will that we can be free. Whereas in fact, as Lucifer well knew, as I know, as you've had intimations, one is only made free by thumbing one's nose at Him."

"And you know at what price that's done."

"The wages of sin is death, but death is likewise the wages of virtue. So you'll need a better bugaboo than that. Hell, perhaps? Why, *this* is hell, nor am I out of it! Dante has no frights for the inmates of Buchenwald. Why didn't your sainted Pope Pius protest the Nazis' ovens? Not through prudence or cowardice, but from an instinct of corporation loyalty. Pius sensed that the deathcamps were the nearest approximation that mortal man has yet made to the Almighty's plan. God is Eichmann writ large."

"Really!" I said. Because there *are* some limits.

"Really," Mordecai insisted. He paced the room faster. "Consider that fundamental organizational principle of the camps—that there be no relation between the prisoners' behavior and their rewards or punishments. In Auschwitz when you do something wrong you're punished, but you're just as likely to be punished when you do as you're told, or even if you do nothing at all. It's quite evident that Gaud has organized His camps on the same model. To quote just one line from Ecclesiastes—a line my mother believed to have a special reference to her own life—'There is a just man that perisheth in his righteousness, and there is a wicked man that prolongeth his life in his wickedness.' And wisdom is of no more use than justice, for the wise man dieth even as the fool.

"We turn our eyes away from the charred bones of children outside the incinerators, but what of a Gaud who damns infants—often the very same one—to everlasting fires? And for, in each case, exactly the same fault—an

69

accident of birth. Believe me, someday Himmler will be canonized. After all, Pius is already. Are you leaving, Sacchetti?"

"I don't want to argue with you, and you leave me little choice. What you say is . . ."

"Unspeakable. For you, perhaps, but not for me. If you'll stay a little longer, though, I'll promise to be more tepid. And I'll reward you—I'll show you where Camp Archimedes is. Not in the Almighty's scheme, but on a map."

"How did you find out?"

"From the stars, like any navigator. You see, an observatory, even a remote-control observatory, has its more prosaic uses too. We're in Colorado. I'll show you."

He took down a folio volume from a shelf and spread it open on his desk. A topographical map of the state covered the two pages. "Here we are," he said, pointing. "Telluride. It was a big mining town at the turn of the century. My theory is that access to the camp is to be had though one of the old mine shafts."

"But if your sightings are all accomplished via television, then you can't be perfectly sure, can you, that the telescope is directly overhead and not a hundred, or a thousand, miles away."

"One is never perfectly sure of anything, but it would seem to be a lot of trouble to no purpose. And besides there was that piece of breccia I picked up off the floor of the catacomb the day before yesterday. It contained traces of sylvanite, one of the gold-bearing tellurides. So, we're in a gold mine *somewhere*."

I laughed, anticipating my own joke: "Performing the magnum opus here is certainly a case of carrying coals to Newcastle."

Mordecai, not laughing (it wasn't such an overwhelming joke, I see now), said: "Quiet! I hear something."

After long silence, I whispered, "What?

Mordecai, his face hidden in his too large hands, made no reply. I was reminded of the first time I'd seen George Wagner, along the darkened stretch of corridor, listening to phantasms. A shudder passed through Mordecai's body, then he relaxed.

"An earth tremor?" he suggested, smiling. "No—no, just

a little inflammation of the imaginative powers, I suppose, like Brother Hugo's. But now you must tell me, honest and true, what do you think of my laboratory? Is it adequate?"

"Oh, it's very fine."

"Could you ever wish for a finer cell to be prisoned in than this?" he asked urgently.

"If I were an alchemist, never."

"It wants nothing, nothing at all?"

"I've read," I said tentatively (for I did not see his purpose in this perfervid questioning), "that some alchemists, in the sixteenth and seventeenth centuries, had seven-piped organs in their laboratories. Music makes cows give more milk. Might it be of any use in your work?"

"Music? I hate music," Mordecai said. "My father was a jazz musician, and my two older brothers. Of the smallest of small times, but it was their life. When they weren't practicing, they'd play records or turn on the radio. I could never open my mouth or make the least sound, but they'd jump on me for it. Don't talk to me about music! Niggers have a natural sense of rhythm, they say, so when I was three years old I had to begin taking tap-dancing lessons. I was lousy at it, and I hated it, but I had this natural sense of rhythm, you see, so the lessons continued. The teacher showed us clippings from old Shirley Temple movies, and we had to learn her routines, right down to the last smile and wink. When I was six, Mammy brought me to the Thursday night talent show at the local theater. She'd dressed me up in this piss-elegant little angel costume, all tinsel and chintz. My number was *I'll Build a Stairway to Paradise*. You know that one?"

I shook my head.

"It goes like this . . ." He began singing the song in his rasping, parroty falsetto and at the same time to shuffle along the carpet.

"Son of a bitch!" he shouted, breaking off. "How the fuck can I do anything on a goddamn rug?" He bent over, caught hold of the tasseled fringe of the figured carpet, and pulled it clear of the tiled floor, dragging along or overturning furniture in the process.

Then he resumed, more loudly, his grotesque song and

71

dance, his arms flailing out of sync with the ill-sung melody. His footwork became mere confused stomping. *"I'm going to get there at any price,"* he shrieked. Flinging both legs out in front of him, he fell on his back. The song degenerated into pained screams, as his arms and legs continued to flail about. He beat his head violently against the tiles of the floor.

The fit had gone on only a short while before the guards arrived with a medical attendant. Mordecai was restrained and sedated.

"You'll have to leave him for a while now," the guards' officer said.

"There's something I was supposed to take with me. If you'll wait just a second."

I went to Mordecai's worktable and found the TOP SECRET folder I'd noticed when Mordecai had spread out the atlas. The officer looked at the folder doubtfully.

"Are you authorized to handle that?" he asked.

"It's a story he wrote," I explained, pulling the typed pages from the folder and showing him the title—Portrait of Pompanianus. "He asked me to read it."

He averted his eyes from the typed pages. "Okay, okay. But don't for Christ's sake *show* it to me!"

I left him then with the medic and the guards. Why is it that whenever I've been with Mordecai I feel, immediately afterward, as though I'd just failed an important examination?

Later:

A note from Mordecai. He has never, he claims, felt better.

June 17

There is great pleasure, and correspondingly great pain (the only metaphor that occurs is dismally anal), in getting out (the metaphor shyly peeps forth) a new oeuvre. Wonderful word, oeuvre.

Louie II's recent intrusion into these pages may prove of benefit in one respect: It has allowed me (compelled me, rather) to look at my past work more clearly, to realize how wholly meretricious it all was . . . and is. I include in this renunciation, I should add, that recent thundergush of rodomontade, *The Hierodule.*

Also, besides the actual Works-in-Progress, I have had glimmerings of something larger, my own magnum opus possibly, which was inspired partly by Mordecai's blasphemies of yesterday. . . .

Have read "Portrait of Pompanianus," which is better than I'd expected, yet curiously disappointing. I think it is because it is so controlled a tale, the plot so meticulously elaborated, the language of such a concinnate beauty, that I'm disgruntled. I'd hoped for a *cri de coeur,* nonobjectivist action-writing, a confidential glimpse of the *real* Mordecai Washington. Whereas R. L. Stevenson might have written "Portrait" as a pendant to "A Lodging for the Night" (except that it is 40,000 words, nearly novel length).

The argument is worth recounting, especially as I've nothing else to fill my journal with today than snippets from the Warping Process (pun, compliments of James Joyce). This, therefore, by way of factoricity:

"Portrait" opens with a razzmatazz set piece in the Rouge-Cloître Monastery, where the mad van der Goes is being treated by the brothers for his "inflammation of the wits." Their remedies are alternately tender and gruesome and uniformly inefficacious. Van der Goes dies in a fit of terror at the inevitability of his damnation.

After the burial (there is a lovely funeral sermon first) a stranger comes in the night, digs up the coffin, opens it, and breathes life back into the corpse. Hugo, we now learn, had sold his soul in exchange for (1) a complete tour of the Italian peninsula to see all the great paintings —the works of Masaccio, Uccelo, della Francesca, et al— known in Flanders only by report or through engravings, and (2) three years of supreme mastery as a painter. It is his ambition not only to surpass the masters of the

73

THOMAS M. DISCH

North and South, but to rival the creations even of the Almighty.

The main body of the story concerns van der Goes' visits to Milan (there is a brief and credible scene with the young da Vinci), Sienna, and Florence. There are long discussions among Hugo, his diabolic companion, and other artists of the time concerning the nature and purpose of art. Van der Goes' initial thesis is the one commonly held: that art should *mirror* reality. He cannot resolve how this may best be done—whether by the microscopic renderings and jewel-like tones of the Flemish school or by the Italianate mastery of space and plastic forms. Gradually, however, as he gains the promised mastery and achieves a synthesis of these two styles, his concern is no longer to mirror reality but (under the devil's instigation) to *compel* it. Art metamorphoses into magic.

Only in his supreme *oeuvre* (as his third year draws to a close), the portrait referred to in the title, does he achieve his supernatural purpose, and even then, as the devil bears him off to hell, the reader is led to doubt whether the catastrophe of the story was a consequence of Hugo's magic or merely of the devil's guile.

There is a rather tepid Faust-Marguerite romance threaded into the plot. I got a chuckle out of the heroine's description: She is modeled, outwardly at least, on Dr. Aimée Busk. No wonder it fails to convince as a romance!

In summary: I liked this book, and I think anybody who likes books about painters and devils would like it too.

Later:
Apart from an hour during dinner, which I ate with the prisoners in the communal dining room (they must get their chef from the Cunard Line!), I've been all day and half the night working . . . at the "larger something" of which I had glimmerings earlier today. It is a drama, my maiden effort in that form, and if sheer speed is any indication of merit, it must be wonderful: I've finished half the first act in a preliminary draft! I almost am afraid to reveal its title. Part of me still recoils from what I am about, like Bowdler confronted with a copy of *Naked Lunch;* another part gasps at the soaring, overreaching

audacity of it. Such tantilizations! Now, I see, I must put up or shut up:

AUSCHWITZ:
A Comedy

Mordecai's "inflammations of the wit" must be contagious. Angels and ministers of grace defend me! I feel possessed!

June 18

Elements of the Quotidian World:

The clocks. The clocks of the corridors, oversize, advertising their manufacturers, straining after neutrality, anxious not to be anxietal, like the clocks in public buildings. However, the minute hand moves not with the slow, imperceptible, downstream flow of other electric timepieces, but with abrupt, unnerving half-minute jumps, quanta of time. The hand is an arrow, but one that has been translated from linear to rotary motion: first the twang of release, followed at once by the dead-sure strike; then for a moment it quivers in its target. One becomes reluctant to inquire the time of such a device.

The absence of natural symbols. To enumerate absences: the sun, and attendant phenomena; colors, any but those *we* have spread upon the walls, or that *we* are wearing, any that *we* have not had to imagine as a condition of their existence; cars or ships or carts or blimps or any *visible* means of transportation (we go everywhere we go in elevators); rain, wind, any of the arbitrary signs of *climate;* a landscape (how rich to the senses would seem even a Nebraska prairie—less, even endless desert), a seascape, a *sky;* trees, grass, soil, *life*—any life but our own dwindling existences. Even such natural symbols as can yet be found among us—such antique simplicities as doors or chairs or bowls of fruit or water jugs or castoff shoes—seem to take on a wholly hypothetical character. Eventually, one supposes, the environment will simply fade away. (This is my observation only by way of confirmation; Barry Meade originated it.)

The dictates of fashion. As if to parody the specious sort of freedom we are allowed here, the prisoners give themselves over to an intemperate and absurd dandyism, avid not so much to dress well as to be on top of whatever *His* or *Time* says is on top. Wigs, spurs, powders, scents, bathing outfits, and ski clothes—anything. Then, as abruptly as these flowers bloomed, they fade; this morning's aesthete becomes the ascetic of the afternoon in a motley, homemade prison garb starker than any self-respecting penitentiary would issue its inmates. The dandyism is, I think, a wistful expression of solidarity with the outside world and with the past; the reaction from it, a declaration of despair that such a solidarity can be achieved.

The cuisine. Food here is unbelievably good. Today, for example, from an immense choice of breakfasts, I had fried bananas, shirred eggs in a peppery tomato sauce, sausages, hot popovers, and capuchino. At noonday, lunching with Barry Meade and the Bishop in the latter's cell, I had a half-dozen Bluepoint oysters, a watercress salad, ortilans on a bed of wild rice, cold asparagus, and, for dessert, a *dame blanche* with soured whipped cream and grenadine. If ever a meal cried out for champagne it was this, but because neither of my lunch partners could or would drink, I settled on Oulmes, a Moroccan mineral water. (If I can't have champagne, I know at least that I'm causing someone a lot of trouble.) The evening meal is the chief social opportunity of the day for most of the prisoners, and no one hurries through it. From the many excellent possibilities, I selected turtle soup; an hors d'oeuvre of sweetbreads; Caesar salad; a rainbow trout, broiled over a wood fire; *rehmedaillon* with a red currant sauce; roasted carrots, French beans with almonds, and a strange puffy kind of potato; and for dessert a double portion of *Wienerschmarm*. (I've been putting on weight as never before, since never before have I had a chance to eat like this day after day—or so little reason to concern myself with my quote figure unquote. I am considered a prodigy by the other prisoners, who have no better appetite than one would expect of condemned men, who are moreover deadly ill. They insist on these banquets in a spirit of perversity: "Let us eat cake!")

The cells. Caprice and costliness are the only common factor. The Bishop, in keeping with his sacerdotal character, is big on ecclesiastical furniture; Meade has a room full of Salvation Army end tables (he is making a movie of them); Murray Sandemann has pedigree Bauhaus antiques. And I have at last taken Mordecai's advice and had my decor altered to suit my taste. The room has been stripped bare, and I live with a cot, a table, and a chair, trying to clothe the nude walls first with stuffs of the imagination, trying to decide. I find, to my chagrin, that I like it just the way it is.

Visiting hours. This journal to the contrary, no one spends much time with anyone else. In the dining hall and certain other areas, promiscuous conversation is tolerated, but it is bad form to address whomever one meets by chance in the library, corridors, etc. Most socializing is conducted on quite formal lines. Guard-delivered invitations with clearly delimited hours are the custom. Everyone is too poignantly aware how short his time is. Everyone can see Time's arrow quivering in the target.

More of this tomorrow perhaps.

Later:
First act of *Auschwitz* completed. Second act under weigh.

June 19

Elements of the Quotidian World (continued):
Movies. Tuesday and Thursday nights. The selection is by majority vote on a list of nominations to which anyone (but not me!) may contribute. In practice, one new movie and one re-run are shown each week. This week's bill: the awesome fragment of Fellini's *Commedia,* which has at

last fought its way out of the Supreme Court; Griffith's film of Ibsen's *Ghosts*. The same actor played both the philandering father and the diseased son. At the end of the last reel a yellow filter is inserted in the projector or, it may be, the film is tinted, and the hero undergoes an attack of locomotor ataxia, hammy but quite unnerving. With *Ghosts*, a number of Terrytoons from the forties and a travelog of mind-wrenching dullness (trout fishing in the Scottish highlands). Why? Not through any sense of camp (no one was laughing). Perhaps this is another abortive effort toward solidarity with the larger world of deadheads outside.

Other entertainments. Since George's death, there has been no resurgence of interest in the theater (though when I've finished *Auschwitz* it may be produced), but occasionally one of the prisoners will give an open reading of his latest work—or a showing, or a whatyoumaycallit Happening. I've been to only one of these, which I found as dull as or duller than *Holiday in Scotland:* an alchemic text in heroic couplets by one of the younger geniuses. Ho hum.

Team sports. Yes, that's what I said. Mordecai, some months ago, invented an elaborate variant of croquet (based partly on Lewis Carroll's game) that is played by teams of three to seven players. Every Friday night there is a tournament between the Columbians and the Unitarians. (The teams' names aren't quite as nicely-nicely as they may seem. They have to do with the rival schools of thought on the question of the nature and origin of syphilis, the Columbian school maintaining that the spirochetes were imported to Europe from the New World by Columbus' sailors—which would account for the great epidemic of 1495—while the Unitarians believe that the many apparent varieties of venereal disease are in fact one, which they call treponematosis, its Protean multiplicity being due to variations of social conditions, personal habits, and climate.)

Anomie. Not surprising, since a lack of vital social or family ties was one of the conditions of the prisoners' selection. Now, it's true, there is a sort of esprit, a community —but it is a community of outcasts, and cold comfort. The exaltations of love, the quieter but more enduring plea-

78

sures of philoprogenitiveness, and the normal, normative happiness of building up, year by year, the form of one's own life, of making that form somehow meaningful, all these—the fundamental human experiences—are denied them, even in possibility. As Meade said regretfully yesterday: "Ah, all those girls I didn't leave behind! The pity of it!" Their genius, though in other respects it may be compensatory, only aggravates the distances that have opened up between them and the common ruck, for even if they were to be cured and allowed to leave Camp Archimedes, they would not find themselves at home in the world. Here in these deep burrows, they have learned to see the sun; there in the world of light, men still watch the shadows on the walls of the cave.

Later:
The second act is done.
Mordecai has another, worse fit today. It may be necessary to postpone the magnum opus. Or as Murray S. calls it, respectfully, the Big Deal.

June 20

Mordecai is well again, and the schedule holds. Have exhausted my capacity for chronicling small beer. Only the waiting now.

Later:
Half of the third act. The thing is fantastic.

June 21

It is fantastic, and it is done!

There's much to revise, of course, but it *is* done. Thanks be to . . .

Whom? Augustine says in his *confessions* (I, 1): "It may come about that the supplicant invoked another in the place of the one he intended—and without knowing it." A danger equally in art as in magic. Well, if the devil must be thanked for *Auschwitz,* then let it be recorded that I thank him and give him his due.

As I write this, it is late afternoon. As I have some time before the dinner hour, I thought I would sketch in a few preliminaries to lighten what may prove a formidable burden of narrative, if the evening is half so eventful as it promises.

In the first giddy moments after I'd written the last speech for *Auschwitz,* when I could suddenly no longer tolerate these bare walls, richer in horrid suggestion than any Rorschach (for hadn't they been the screen upon which I had projected the successive images of my dismal comedy?), I stumbled out into the hypogeal daedal of corridors, happening across the hidden heart of it, or its minotaur at least, Haast. Who, himself giddy with his improbable expectations, invited me to accompany him to the little fane, four levels down, that had lately been the scene of *Faustus* and which is to be the catacomb for tonight's solemn mysteries.

"Excited?" he asked, though really it was a declaration of fact.

"Aren't you?"

"In the Army a man has to learn to live with excitement. Besides, being as confident as I am of the outcome . . ." He smiled weakly, expressing confidence, and waved me into the elevator.

"No, the real excitement won't start until certain of-

80

ficers in certain Pentagon offices hear about what I've accomplished. No need to name names. It's common knowledge that for twenty years a small but powerful clique in Washington has been burning up millions and billions of taxpayers' dollars to get us into Outer Space. While all of *Inner* Space had yet to be explored."

Then, when I wouldn't rise to the bait: "You must be wondering what I mean by that expression—*Inner* Space?"

"It's a very . . . thought-provoking . . ."

"It's my own idea, and it relates to what I was explaining to you the other day, concerning the materialism of modern-day science. You see, science accepts only *material* facts, whereas in fact Nature always has *two* sides, a material and a spiritual. Just as every human being has two sides, a Body and a Soul. The body is the product of the dark, shadowy earth, and in alchemy this is what must be *albified,* that is to say, made as white as a naked, shining sword." As though questing for the hilt of this sword, his hands waved about oratorically.

"Now the materialist scientist lacks this fundamental insight, and so *his* whole attention is directed to Outer Space, whereas an alchemist is always aware of the importance of *teamwork* between Body and Soul, and so he's naturally more interested in Inner Space. I could write a whole book about it . . . if only I had your gift for words."

"Oh, books!" I said, hastening to dampen these ardors. "There's a lot more important things than books. As the Bible says, 'Of making many books, there is no end.' A life of action can contribute more good to society than—"

"I don't need *you* to tell me that, Sacchetti. I haven't wasted *my* life in some ivory tower. But still, the book I have in mind would be no ordinary piece of trash. It could answer many of the questions that are disturbing thoughtful people these days. If you'd care to look at some of the notes I've made . . . ?"

Seeing that he was not to be stopped, I relinquished to him with grudging grace. "That would be interesting."

"And maybe you could advise me on how I can improve them. I mean, to make them clearer to the average reader."

I nodded gloomily.

"And maybe—"

I was spared this last turn of the thumbscrew by our arrival at the entrance to the sanctum simultaneously with Dr. Aimée Busk.

"You're a bit early," Haast told her. His emissile good fellowship retracted like a snail's cornua at the sight of Busk—in a suit as gray and chaste as any flatworm, epalpibrate, grimly mounted on her iron heels and ready to ride to battle.

"I've come to inspect the equipment that will be used at the séance. With your permission?"

"There are already two electronics experts going over every circuit. But if you think they need *your* advice . . ." He made a stiff bow, and she preceded him into the theater, saluting trimly.

The flats for the first and last acts of *Faustus* had not been stripped, and the soaring bookshelves and shadowed staircase served now as a backdrop for the new drama. A lectern carved in the form either of an eagle or an angel supported a fat leather volume, a real book this, not mere painted canvas. It was spread open to a page of such cabalistic scribblings as I'd noticed on Mordecai's desk, but whether this was a further theatricality or of some pragmatic and sacramental significance I could not tell.

This much accorded well with traditional presentations of *Faustus;* the elements added since seemed more suited to a modern horror movie, a ragtag, Japanese version of *Frankenstein* perhaps. There were bubblers in assorted colors, like giant Christmas tree ornaments, and what might have been a war surplus telescope, the larger end focused, introspectively, on the floorboards. There was a battery of dials and winkers and spinning reels of tape, homage to the cult of Cybernetick. But the happiest inspiration of the set designer had been a pair of modified hair driers whence burgeoned, as from cornucopiae, a rich profusion of electrical spaghetti. Two N.S.A. engineers were inspecting the tangled innards of these perfect little orange plastic and chrome deathseats, while the Bishop watched over them to preserve the circuitry against sacrilege. They nodded to Busk, recognizing her.

"Well?" she asked. "How are our black boxes? Will they turn everything they touch to gold?"

One of the engineers laughed uneasily. "As far as we can tell, Doctor, they don't do a damned thing except hum."

"It seems to me," Busk said, addressing me and pretending to have forgotten Haast, "that if one were setting out to perform magic tricks, one wouldn't need much more than a chalk circle and a dead chicken. Or, at the very most, an orgone box."

"There's no need to become filthy," Haast said sullenly. "You'll see what they can do when the time comes. People made fun of Isaac Newton the same way, because he studied astrology. You know what he said to them? He said, 'Sir, I have studied it, you have not.'"

"Newton, like most geniuses of any size, was a nut. Madness is becoming to a genius, but I find it surprising that a man like yourself, a pedestrian, should need to go so far afield for the elements of his neurosis. Especially in view of the old saw, 'Once bitten, twice shy.'" She desired not argument but, like a picador, simply to wound.

"Are you talking about Auaui? What everybody seems to forget about that campaign is that I won it. Despite the diseases, despite the treason of my staff, I won it. Despite the *lies* that surround me and despite, let me add, the most unfavorable horoscopes I've ever had to deal with, I won it!"

Wrinkling her nose with pleasure at the scent of blood, she stood back and determined where to place the next pic. "I've been unfair," she said, carefully. "Because I'm sure that Berrigan was much more responsible for all that happened there than you, as responsibility is judged these days. Please excuse me."

She must have thought, as I did, that this would have brought him to an entire standstill, ready for the banderilleros. But not at all. He walked to the lectern and then, as though reading from the hierograms in the book, said, "Say what you will."

Busk lifted a minuscule eyebrow, inquiringly.

"Say what you will—there's something in it." He thwacked the lectern soundly with his fist. Then, with his inimitable sense of catechesis, he quoted the epigraph of Berrigan's book: "There are more things in heaven and

THOMAS M. DISCH

earth, Horatio, than are dreamt of in your philosophy."

No wonder the man wins all his battles: He doesn't recognize defeat!

Busk reined in her lips and galloped off. When she was gone, Haast, smiling, turned to me. "Well, we sure showed old Siegfried, didn't we? Take my advice, Louie—never try and argue with a woman."

Traditionally these comic episodes are prelude to more terrible events: Hamlet mocks Polonius, the Fook makes riddles, the drunken porter stumbles across the stage to answer the knocking at the gate.

Later:

I did not expect the catastrophe so soon. The play is all but over, and I'd thought we were somewhere in the middle of the second act. There is nothing left to be done now but to bear the bodies from the stage.

As always, I was in my seat well before curtain time, though not in advance of Haast, who as I came in was worrying the maintenance crew about the ventilators, which had developed a sudden autism. He had shaved the afternoon's white stubble from his face and changed into a black double-breasted suit. Though of the latest cut, the suit seemed dated. Visiting Stuttgart in the early sixties I'd noticed how many of the businessmen were wearing the styles of their youth; for them—and for Haast—it would always be 1943.

The few prisoners not playing an active role in the rites arrived next, some in formal wear, others in their electic but no less sober attire. They took their seats not *en bloc* but scattered throughout the small auditorium so that when they were settled the theater seemed scarcely less empty than it had been.

Busk too had chosen to dress as though in mourning. She took the seat behind mine, and began immediately chain-smoking Camels. In a short while she had woven a little cocoon of smoke about the two of us, aided by the vents' malfunction.

Mordecai, the Bishop, and a small host of censers, ostiaries, etc. (looking like the first act of *Tosca* at the Amato Opera) arrived last, or rather, they entered, with oleaginous pomp. The Bishop was goldenly decked out in Matis-

84

sely symbolatrous vestments, though even he preserved one touch of the funereal. His mitre was dead black. Mordecai had exercised a certain macabre economy in choosing his costume for the ball: It was the same black velvet suit with a gold lace collar that George Wagner had worn as Faust. It stood all too evidently in need of dry cleaning, but even fresh it would have been wrong on Mordecai, whom it caused to seem almost uniformly black. Worse, its cut emphasized the narrowness of his chest, his rounded back and bandy legs, his ungainliness walking as much as his gracelessness in repose. He resembled, on an enlarged scale, one of Velasquez's pathetic dwarfs, the rich costume serving only to set off the grotesque frame. This was, doubtless, the effect intended. Pride will flaunt its ugliness quite as if it were beauty.

Haast hurried to this monkey Hamlet and grasped him, albeit gingerly, by the hand. "This is a historic occasion, my boy." His voice was husky with deeply felt self-importance.

Mordecai nodded, removing his hand. His eyes shone with a fierce attentiveness, uncustomary even for him. I was reminded of van der Goes' "painful eyes" in "Portrait of P." "Thirsty for light, his gaze would keep returning to the sun."

The Bishop, duly ceremonious and followed by two supernumeraries who supported the glittering cope, preceded Haast up the four steps to the stage. Mordecai lingered in the aisle, scanning the faces in the audience. When his eyes met mine, there was a sudden flicker of amusement. He came along the front row to my seat, stooped, and whispered:

"Now I want
Spirits to enforce, art to enchant;
And my ending is despair.
Unless I be reliev'd by prayer."

He rose, crossing his arms, over the stained velvet, smug. "Do you know who said that? I can see that you don't— but you *should*."

"Who?"

He went to the steps, mounted the first, and turned. "It was the same who said, earlier

> "I'll break my staff,
> Bury it certain fadoms in the earth—"

I finished, interrupting him, Prospero's farewell to his magic arts:

> "And deeper than did ever plummet sound
> I'll drown my book."

"But not, you know," Mordecai added with a wink, *"just* yet."

Haast, who was waiting at the lectern for Mordecai to come up on the stage, rattled a handful of crisp papers at us impatiently. "What are the two of you jabbering about? We shouldn't be talking now—we should be preparing our minds, emptying them out for a great spiritual experience. You don't seem to realize that we stand on a brink."

"But I do, I do!" Mordecai took the three steps in one unsteady stride, crossed the stage at a brisk hobble, and took a seat beneath one of the Medusalike driers. Immediately Sandemann began fixing wires to his forehead with adhesive.

"I'm dumb," he said. "Commence."

Haast laughed delightedly. "Well, I certainly didn't mean to imply that. But nevertheless . . ." He turned back to his meager audience. "Before we begin, ladies and gentlemen, there are one or two things I'd like to say. Concerning the great undertaking that is about to transpire." Then he began to read from the typescript in his hand.

Busk leaned forward to whisper stagily: "I'll bet the old gerontophobe goes on half an hour. He's afraid to bring it to a test. He's afraid of his silly brink."

He exceeded her estimate by fifteen minutes. Though I pride myself on the circumstantiality of this record I will not give more than the briefest synopsis here of that speech. Haast spoke first of the satisfaction it afforded him to be a benefactor of mankind and provided capsule accounts of the lives and contributions of earlier benefactors: Christ, Alexander the Great, Henry Ford, and the great modern astrologer Carl Jung (pronounced with a soft J). He described affectingly the pathos and terror of aging and demonstrated how much harm is done to the social organism by the continual chopping off of its most experienced and useful members by short-sighted compulsory retirement programs and death. He revealed the principle by which the Soul can remain forever youthful ("Keep an open mind, and be receptive to Fresh Approaches"), but he confessed that it had been the despair of his mature years that he could not find the complementary principle by which the body might preserve like agelessness. Then, in just these last few months, he had, aided by his young colleagues (with the briefest of nods toward Mordecai) rediscovered a secret known centuries before to a privileged few but soon to be confided, if not universally, then to all members of society responsible enough to be able to benefit by it: the secret of eternal life.

By the time he was done I had become somewhat dizzied by the thick smoke about me and the growing heat. It must have been even hotter onstage, under the lights, for both Haast and the Bishop had become quite luminous with sweat.

While Haast, in turn, was being strapped and fitted beneath the drier, the Bishop advanced to the lectern and asked us to join him in a short prayer specially composed for the occasion.

Busk rose to her feet. "Pray until midnight, it's your production. But might I ask you, as we seem to have abundant time, the *purpose* of these various devices? Alchemists of the classic era must certainly have got by with simpler artifacts. When I asked the same question of two engineers this afternoon, they were unable to enlighten me, or themselves, and so I had hoped that you . . .?"

"What you ask is not easy," the Bishop replied, with an affected and ludicrous gravity. "You seek to understand in moments what it has taken mankind untold centuries to comprehend. Is it the anachronism of electronics that puzzles you? But surely it would be short-sighted not to avail ourselves of *all* the resources of science! Because we respect the wisdom of the ancients

87

does not mean that we must despise the technical virtuosity of our own age."

"Yes, yes, yes—but what does it *do?*"

"Essentially . . ." He furrowed his brow. "Essentially, it magnifies. Though in another sense you might say that it accelerates. In its traditional form, the form known to Paracelsus, the elixir is slow-working. Once it has been absorbed into the bloodstream, it begins to penetrate the three meninges—the dura mater, the arachnoid, and the pia mater. Only when these have been wholly transmogrified by the elixir—and this period increases in direct proportion to age or ill health—only then does the process of corporeal rejuvenation begin. But clearly, we could not afford a philosophic patience. We needed to hasten the action of the elixir, and that is the purpose of the equipment you see here."

"*How* does it achieve this purpose?"

"Ah, that question takes us into deeper waters. First, the alpha pickup—that is, the device being readied now for Mr. Haast—records and analyzes the electroencephalographic patterns. These records are then in turn processed by—"

"Enough idle talk!" Haast shouted, pushing aside Sandemann, who was fixing the wire coronet to his perspiring brow. "She's already heard more than she's cleared for. Jesus Christ Almighty, you people don't have any sense of Security! If she talks up again, I want the guards to remove her from the auditorium. Is that understood? Now, let's get back to business."

Once again Sandemann began taping the wires to Haast, working with the nervous, finicking methodicalness of a barber shaving a restless customer. Mordecai, his eyes hidden under the drier, was picking at his teeth with a fingernail. Boredom? Bravado? Tension? Without being able to glimpse his eyes I could not interpret.

The Bishop, adding some vibrato, now commenced his prayer, which (he pointed out) had been adapted from a prayer of the fourteenth century alchemist Nicholas Flamel:

"Almighty God, father of light waves, from Whom flow, as blood from a beating heart, all further benisons, we beseech Thy infinite mercy. Grant that we may share

88

in that eternal wisdom that surrounds Thy throne, which created and perfected all things, which leads them to their fulfillment or annihilation. Thine is the wisdom that governs the celestial and occult arts. Grant, Abbas, that that wisdom may shine forth upon our works, that we may proceed unerring in that noble art to which we dedicate our spirits, seeking that miraculous stone—"

At this point one of the supernumeraries, kneeling at the side of the stage, rang a silvery bell.

"That stone of the sages—"

Two bells, in chorus.

"That most precious stone, which Thou in Thy wisdom hast hidden from the tellurian world, but which Thou canst reveal to Thy elect."

Three—and as they jingled solemnly, the doors swung open and the philosophical egg, looking more than ever like a great cooking pot, was wheeled into the room atop a small battery-powered trolley. Four supers lifted it to the stage.

Busk leaned forward to risk a small sneer. "Rituals! I'll take a good honest compulsion neurosis any day." But there was an overinsistence in the statement and in her manner which suggested that the Bishop's gallimaufrey was having its effect even on her—perhaps, indeed, especially on her.

Dizzy with the burning Camels and attacked by bellycrabs as well, I found my attention straying from the prayer to the brute business of unsealing the egg, which was taking place almost directly above me. Only when this was accomplished did the Bishop's viscid incantations emerge from the humming darkness of the Latinate into the realm of ordinary humbug, just as sometimes, in a supermarket or elevator, one recognizes the tune playing on the Muzak.

". . . and just as Thy only begotten Son is at once God and man, just as He, born without sin and not subject to death's dominion, chose to die that we might be free of sin and live eternally in His presence, just as He rose glorious on the third day, just so is the Carmot, philosophic gold, without sin, ever the same and radiant, able to survive all trials, yet ready to die for its ailing and imperfect brothers. The Carmot, gloriously born anew, delivers them, tinctures them for life eternal, and bestows on them the consubstantial perfection of the state of pure gold. So do we now, in the name of that same Christ Jesus, ask of Thee this food of angels, this miraculous cornerstone of heaven, set in place for all eternity, to govern and reign with Thee, for Thine is the kingdom, and the power, and the glory, for ever and ever."

Even Busk joined in the response. "Amen."

The Bishop, handing his crozier to a super, approached the decanted egg and lifted out the earthen bottle that had been baking inside these forty days and nights. The lights were cut on cue, all but a single spot focused through the telescopic do-thingy I'd seen that afternoon. (This light, I was later informed, was derived—by an unspecified process—from the star Sirius.) The Bishop poured the murky contents into a chalice, which, filled to the brim, he elevated into the beam of pure Sirian light. Now the assembled prisoners, on stage and off, perpetrated their most audacious plagiarism. They began to sing Aquinas' Eucharistic hymn, "O esca viatorum."

> *"O esca viatorum,*
> *O panis angelorum,*
> *O manna caelitum . . ."*

At the climax of his purloined ceremony, the Bishop turned and offered the chalice to the lips first of Haast, then of Mordecai, both so swaddled in electrical gear that they could barely incline the chalice to drink from it. As each drank, the Bishop recited his own execrable translation from Aquinas' crisp Latin:

"O food of wayfarers! Bread of angels! Manna wherewith all heaven's fed! Draw nigh and with thy sweetness sate the heart that ever hungers for thee."

The last spot faded to black, and we waited in that tepid, unmoving air for what we all feared, even the most sanguine and self-deluded.

It was Haast's voice, though strangely altered, that broke the stillness. "Give me some light! Lights! It works, I can feel it—I can feel the change!"

The full complement of spots came on, dazzling the retina's mild rods. Haast stood center stage, having torn

90

the crown of wires from his scalp. Blood trickled from his temple and down his sweating, suntanned face, which gleamed in the spotlights like buttered toast. Trembling throughout his body, he threw open his arms and exulted in his reedy voice: "Look, you bastards! Look at me— I'm young again. My whole body is alive! Look!"

But our eyes were not on Haast. Mordecai, who had not stirred all this while, now with painful slowness lifted his right hand before his eyes. He made a sound that mourned all hope, that raised misery to the exquisiteness of mortal terror, and when his rigid frame would not support this outburst any longer, he cried aloud: "Black! The blackness! All, all black!"

It was over without transition. The body slumped in the chair, though the entangling wires prevented it from falling to the floor. A doctor from the infirmary had been waiting in attendance in the corridor. His diagnosis was almost as abrupt as Mordecai's death.

"But how?" Haast shouted at him. "How *could* he die?"

"An embolism, I should say. I'm not surprised. At this stage the smallest excitement might have been enough." The doctor turned back to Mordecai, now lying on the floor, as graceless in death as in life, and closed his wide-opened eyes.

Haast smiled strickenly. "No! You're lying again. He's not dead, he's *not*, he can't be. *He* drank the elixir too. He's been *restored* to life, reborn, albified! Life is eternal!"

Busk rose to her feet, laughing abusively. "Youth!" she jeered. "And eternal life, is it? Is this how it works, your elixir of youth?" And with the bull of magic dead before her, she strode out of the theater, confident that she had merited ears and tail.

Haast pushed the doctor away from the corpse and laid his hand over its stilled heart. His groan was the brother of that which had shattered the body at his feet.

He stood up, eyes closed, and spoke, at first almost somnambulistically, then with mounting shrillness. "Take him. Take him from this room. Cremate him! Take him to the furnace now, and burn him. Burn him till there are only ashes! Oh, the black traitor! I'll *die* now, and it's him that will be to blame. I'm no younger—it was a trick. It

91

was always a trick. Damn him! Damn the black bastard! Damn him, damn him, damn him forever!" And with each "Damn," Haast kicked the corpse's head and chest.

"Please, sir! Think of your own health!"

Haast retreated at the doctor's restraining touch, as though in fear. Stumbling backward, his hand came down upon the lectern for support. Quietly but systematically, Haast tore pages from the book and threw them on the floor. "Lies," he said, crumpling the thick paper. "More lies. Treasons. Deception. Lies."

The prisoners seemed strangely to disregard Mordecai's body, which the guards, just arriving, had thrown on the trolley that had brought in the philosophical egg. It had proven to be no more, after all, than the most commonplace Dutch oven. I took a handkerchief from my pocket to wipe the blood from his face, but too soon the guards had my arms. As they led me out, Haast was still ripping apart the drowned, drowned book.

June 22

Waking in the middle of the night, I recorded, in sleepy shorthand, the nightmare that had awakened me, then fell back into bed, longing for the numbness at the end of thought, and lay there, hollow and dry, staring into uncompassionate darkness. This, elaborated from those notes, is my dream.

There was first a scent of cloying sweetness, as of rotting fruit. I realized it was coming from the large hole in the center of the room. A very fat man was standing at the bottom of this hole amid heaps of breccia. Tonsured, a monk. His hood and habit were white: a Dominican.

He took the cord girdling his middle and tossed one end to me. Pulling him out was an almost impossible task. At last, though, we both sat at the edge of the hole, gasping.

"Usually, of course," he said, "I can float. Often to the height of a cubit."

For so gross a man he seemed oddly insubstantial. Gaseous almost. The pudgy hands resembled rubber gloves blown up to bursting. I thought to myself: Louis, if you don't watch it, pretty soon this is what you'll look like.

"And that's only a single miracle. I could mention many others. *Quantam sufficit,* as Augustine observes. Have you nowhere I can sit?"

"My chairs, I'm afraid, would be rather too . . . secondary. Perhaps the bed?"

"And something to eat. A little bread, some herrings." He jabbed a fist-balloon at the springs. "I've come to deliver a message. Consequently, I shall not stay long."

I pushed the button beside the door. "A message for me?"

"A message from God." He lowered himself onto the rumpled sheets. The hood shadowed all but the lower part of his face, where his mouth should have been.

"I doubt it," I said, as politely as I could.

"Doubt God? Doubt He exists? What nonsense! Of course you believe in God—everybody does. I myself have proven his existence three different ways. First, if He didn't exist, everything would be entirely different. Up would be down, and right would be left. But we see that this is not the case. Ergo, God must exist. Secondly, if God did not exist neither of us would be here now, waiting for something to eat. Thirdly, we have only to look at our watches to see that He exists. What time is it?"

"A bit past three."

"Oh dear, oh dear. They're *very* late. Are you good at riddles? Why did the hyperdulia pray to the Pia Mater?"

"Why is a raven like a writing desk?" I mumbled, beginning to be annoyed with my guest. I don't think he heard me, or if he did, he failed to grasp the allusion.

"You don't know! Here's another. A teacher of mine said, 'You call him a dumb ox. But I tell you that this dumb ox shall bellow so loud that his bellowing will fill the world.' Who am I?"

"Thomas Aquinas?"

"*Saint* Thomas Aquinas. You should have known that right off. Are you dumb?"

93

"Not compared to most."

"Compared to most—but what about compared to me? Ha! And God is smarter even than I. He is at the pinnacle of the chain of being. He is the first and *immaterial* being, and as intellectuality is a result of immateriality, it follows as the night the day that He is the first intelligent being. Have you read Dionysius?"

"I'm afraid not."

"You should, you should. It was he who wrote that each order of heavenly being is taught divine science by the highest minds. As, for example, *I* teach *you*. Abbot Suger was especially keen on Dionysius. What did I just say?"

"What?"

"Say what I just said back to me. You can't. If you won't listen to simple things, how shall I be able to give you the message?"

There was a knock at the door. It was the coffee cart, but metamorphosed from tarnished chrome to blazing gold and studded thickly with precious stones. Three small angels, no bigger than kindergartners, brought it through the door, two pulling from the front, one pushing from behind. I wondered why they didn't fly, whether perhaps their little wings were aerodynamically unsound, as I remembered having read in a popular science magazine.

One cherub removed a tray of small, rotting fish from the bottom of the cart. He arranged these in a handsome Spode bowl and brought it to the saint, who had cupped his hands to receive it, a gesture of beatitude. As the cherub passed by me, a wingtip brushed my face. It was made not of feathers but of fine, white fur.

"A miracle! Every meal is a little miracle, you know. Herrings especially. I died from eating miraculous herrings." He took three of the fish in his bloated fingers and shoved them into the shadow of his hood. "A peddlar came by the monastery with a load of sardines. I'm not very fond of sardines, but herring—ah, herring is another matter! And what do you think happened? He looked into his last cask"—another handful of the decayed fish went in, scarcely interrupting the anecdote—"and it was full of herring! A miracle if there ever was one. Except that,

94

as it turned out, they were spoiled, and I died three days later, after the most excruciating stomach cramps you can imagine. Isn't that fantastic? The story of my life would make a book. You wouldn't believe some of the things. Though there would be very little of"—he cleared his throat and handed the empty bowl back to the angel —"of a carnal nature. Because from the age of twenty I never experienced an impulse of the flesh. Not once. It made my studies immeasurably easier."

Another cherub approached with a golden tray of pastries, from which Aquinas selected a chocolate éclair. Only now did I notice the distressing inflammations that had swollen the cherub's tiny scrotum and caused the poor thing to walk with a strange, straddling gait. My guest caught my look.

"It's the orchitis, you know," he said, biting into the éclair, which squirted whipped cream from its other end. "Inflammation of the testicles. From the Greek, ὄρχις, or testicle, whence also the word orchid, because of the shape of its tubers. It all comes back to the same thing, sex, S-E-X. This is excellent pastry." The éclair consumed, he helped himself to a piece of cheesecake from the tray.

"You've read, of course, about how my brother Raynaldo by my mother's orders, had me abducted and brought to the tower of Roccasecca to be held prisoner there in order that I might not fulfill my vocation. Raynaldo was determined to take the tempter's part and he sent a young lady to my cell, a blond girl of remarkable charm, for I couldn't help remarking on it even as I chased her out with a flaming brand. I burnt the sign of the cross into the wood of the door to prevent her return. and it was then that the divine mercy issued the happy dispensation I have already spoken of. That is the tale that has always been told, but there is a sequel to it not so generally known. Raynaldo sought to undermine my constancy by more than that one device. At that time I was considered not unfavored in my physical person. I was slim as once even you, Sacchetti, were slim, a very atomy, and I moved with a leopard's grace. But in that close prison I could not move at all. I read—the Bible and the Master of the Sentences—and wrote—one or two inconsequent, opuscula—and prayed. But, also, and necessarily, I ate.

Hunger is as powerful an impulse of the flesh as con-
cupiscence, and even more basic to our animal nature. I
ate four and sometimes five meals a day. Savory meats
and delicate sauces and the most exquisite little cakes,
far surpassing *this*, were prepared in a kitchen that was
engaged solely in making my meals. Once, twice, I refused
my food, threw it from the window or trampled it on the
floor, but then Raynaldo would starve me out. He would
keep all food from me for three, four, five days, until it
was Friday or a day of fast, and then there would be, ah,
the most thrilling and abundant foods. I could not, I *could*
not resist, then, or—later. After I escaped Roccasecca I
found that on all the fast days of the calendar I would
be revisited by an insatiable, tormenting hunger. I could
not pray, I could not read, I could not think, until that
hunger had been assuaged. And thus, as through the
years the immaterial intellect expanded like some godlike,
moist squash, my material and fleshly aspect, my body, by
its crapulence, did swell and magnify to . . . this!" He
threw up his hood, revealing what must once have been his
face. Gluttony had so overwhelmed it as to blot out all
features but the heavy sag of jowls and chin that sur-
rounded the stained orifice of the mouth. More than a face
the pasty flesh resembled a vast buttocks, in which the
eyes were the merest dimples.

"And now I suppose you'd like some cake too. Oh, I
saw the greedy look you gave that pastry tray. Mopsy,
the time is at hand—bring Mr. Sacchetti his message."

As his two fellows caught hold of my arms and pulled
me to my knees, the third rabbit-headed cherub approached me, wiggling his tiny pink nose with the pleasure
of anticipation, its furry wings fluttering spasmodically,
like the beating of a defective heart. With chubby fingers
it reached into the flowerlike and suppurating wound of its
scrotum and withdrew thence a thin white host covered
with indecipherable script.

"I'm afraid . . . that I don't . . . understand."

"You must eat it, of course," Thomas Aquinas explained.
"Then your understanding will be as a god's."

The cherub forced the bread (which smelled of that
same odor that had earlier risen from the pit) into my
mouth. Releasing me, the angels burst into song:

"O esca viatorum
O panis angelorum
O manna cáelitum

Esurientes ciba,
Dulcédine non priva,
Corda quaerentium."

As the nauseating sweetness spread through my mouth, the message, like a lamp burning miraculous oils, dazzled me with its insupportable truth.

"How could I not have known!"

I could see our names in giant letters of azure and gold, as clearly as in any book: George Wagner's first; then Mordecai's, and all the other prisoners' in a monotonous progression; and there at the bottom of the page, my own.

But the pain lay not in this, but in the certainty that I *had* known. I had known almost since my arrival at Camp Archimedes.

Aquinas rolled on the floor with laughter, a limbless sowbelly stomach pumping blood into a great horned pumpkin of a head. His bellowing filled the room, blotting out the angels' gentle carol, and I woke.

Later:

Haast, under pressure, confirms what it is no longer in any case possible to conceal, which had been kept from me this long only by my own desperate, deliberate blindness. Now that I do know it, now that I *know* I know it, I feel an actual relief, like a murderer whose case has dragged on for weeks and who hears his verdict at last, the verdict that had never been in doubt—"Guilty"—and, with the same sureness, his sentence, "Death." It was not a dream, and the message was true. I have been, since May 16, infected with the Pallidine. Everyone here had known but I, and I, though I would not listen to the whispers until they were a bellowing that filled the world, I had known too.

97

BOOK TWO

[The following notes, set off by asterisks, are reproduced as they appear in Louis Sacchetti's journal. They are in the order in which they were written, but aside from this we have only internal evidence by which to date them. Thus, the first mention of Skilliman (in the twelfth note) would suggest that this, and succeeding, entries could have been written no earlier than the ninth of August. By their manner we may also safely suppose that the three concluding notes (beginning at "More and more, it is in *his* gardens that we walk"), which occupy the bulk of this section of the journal, were written toward the end of this period, just before Sacchetti resumed work on a regular (and may we also say intelligible?) basis; this would give us the twenty-eighth of September as a terminal date for these "ravings" (as their author himself styles them later). Much of the following material is not original with Sacchetti, but where he has not himself cited his sources— and he does not, usually, bother—we have not presumed to do so, if only because it would be too large an undertaking and of small interest to any but specialists. Among his sources we may list: the Bible, Aquinas, the Kabbalah, various alchemic texts, including the second part of *The Romance of the Rose,* Richard (and George) Wagner, Bunyan, Milton, de Lautréamont, Rilke, Rimbaud, and any number of modern English poets. Ed.]

* *

"Too much introspection. Not enough factoricity. Concentrate on vivid descriptions of real things." He's right, I know. My only excuse—that hell is murky.

* *

The belly of the whale—or of the stove?

* *

"He heard doleful voices and rushings to and fro, so that sometimes he thought he would be torn in pieces, or trodden down like mire in the streets." Then, a bit farther on: "Just when he was come over against the mouth of the burning pit, one of the wicked ones got behind him, and stepped up softly to him, and whisperingly suggested many grievous blasphemies to him, which he verily thought had proceeded from his own mind. . . . He had not the discretion neither to stop his own ears nor to know from whence those blasphemies came."

Bunyan.

* *

We pretend that art redeems the time; in truth, it only passes it.

* *

"Whatsoever the Lord pleased, He hath done." A dire truth.

* *

"His life then began to take on the aspect of a glass of water, of the sort in which he would rinse his brushes: the several colors, mingling, were the color of mud."

"Portrait of P."

* *

It is because of the wooden tub that one believes so readily in the angel beside it, the angel that plays a cello.

* *

What Mordecai said about "Portrait": "It is dull, but then its very dullness is part of its interest. I am not dull on purpose, but rather I allow the dull passages to fall where they will."

And, another time: "Art *must* court tedium. One man's still-life is another's *nature morte*."

* *

The pebbles, grating beneath my iron heels, are the charred bones of children.

* *

Do not earn, do not spend,
Do not worry, friend:
Time must have an end.
Hurry! Hurry!

* *

Here in hell the choice is only between the deepest cold and the extremest heat. "Between these two states they flee roaring to and fro, for in the one the other always seems heavenly refreshment."

* *

Of Haast, Skilliman says: "A mind so innately disordered that he would be hard put to arrange the letters of the alphabet in a sequence."

* *

So! Even the alphabet is crumbling. As though some squalling, nasty child were to strike down a castle of painted blocks.
Skilliman's infantile face.

* *

The Parable of the Pumpkin and the Hollyhocks
That spring in the middle of his hollyhocks there grew an intellectual pumpkin. The hollyhocks were beautiful, but he knew the pumpkin would be more useful. It didn't ripen until October, by which time the hollyhocks had already been eaten.

* *

"I knew a man who wrote seven good poems in a single evening."
"Seven in one night! It's hard to believe."

* *

103

Without science we wouldn't have these rows of up-risen stelae. It (science) is a veil over open lips, it is the word unspoken. Even the damned are reverent at that altar.

* *

Amfortas' lament has become my own:

Nie zu hoffen
dass je ich könnte gesunden.

* *

A Sebastian, wounded by Time's arrow.

* *

Meade said: "But in other ways, Skilliman isn't such a bad sort. His eyes, for instance, are quite nice—if you like eyes."

It is a joke that carries me back to the limits of memo-ry—to high school. Poor Barry—he's literally falling to pieces. As though his body were impatient for its autopsy.

And later he said: "My senses are losing their touch."

* *

Today Skilliman, in a fit of temper, invented this verse, called

The Earth
It'd be more perfect as a smooth sphere
With God's good oceans everywhere.

* *

"Birds of a strange nature, high-shouldered, with crooked bills, were standing in the muck, and looking motionlessly to one side."

Mann.

* *

104

"This isn't Democracy; this is humor."
Vito Battista.

* *

A new inscription for Hellgate: *Here everything leaves off.*

* *

Someday in our colleges Himmler will be studied. The last of the great chiliasts. The landscapes of his interior world will elicit only an *agreeable* amount of terror. (Of Beauty, therefore.) Consider that the transcripts of the atrocity trials are already, these many years, offered for our entertainment in theaters. *Beauty is nothing but the beginning* ...

* *

More and more, it is in *his* gardens that we walk. Who, if I cried out *then*, who would hear? Mute overthrown-ness! (Chirico)

Horror smiled at the angels, at all of them ... appalling-ly. We who have been waiting for just this can admire the illusion. "Why, it looks exactly like fire!"

Who is there to answer to the sky? A soul: it is done, it happens. Ill with fantasizing, with reckoning in words, with soundless meanings. *It happens to all eternity*. They call every day, each to the other. Lips forced to use the brains, against all delicacy. Suspicions and foul oaths—oh, the very foulest! Yea, the morning stops!

Oh, and the nights—the nights will torment and excite. A lust of shame stands and inhabits us. We gnaw and nibble then at the extremities of filthiness. It leaves, as on a wind ... but windless. Winding down the cold, the dark streets. (The cobbles bubbling in the heat.) They rush roaring to and fro on golden sidewalks, toward the lifting horizon. An illusion!

Interior, arterial jungles, whence the Spirit rushes. The enchantment collapsing in on itself, expiring with a mighty sneeze. Boys there waiting in line to die, grumbling,

105

patient. Their blood flutters into me. Ravines from which the Spirit departs, like a glutted condor. Posts of this prison universe; troops rocketing off to face (by preference) every Terror. What Lucifer whispers of, some mornings.

The sin of death spares the sons of David. Hope is a swampland under a glouting sky. A prehistoric wilderness of island-nights. Hinges of cell-mud. Hell grows, joylessly, out of the testes of the dying. (Whispers: Oh, the lecherous thickets of death!) O Mephistopheles!

The deathcamps: fat, swollen, blossoming exorbitantly. Roots sucking at the ground made ready by the Almighty's plan. (Only He *can*.)

God? God is our F——er; and here between the floating flowers, mental organizational principles. These, birds of a strange nature, existing between behavior and reward. Standing in the muck, looking *at something wrong*, eyes slightly askew, as in an old woodcut.

"You are punished with stalks of bamboo," he says. You do as you're told. . . . He felt his heart knocking against the god that had organized this camp. Ecclesiastes.

* *

My entrails are trodden down like mire in the streets. My limbs deform and prostrate me. Rushings to and fro! up and down! "I have swallowed a monstrous dose of——!"

Dreadful noises slide by like "fish." It is hell, eternal punishment, where he thought he heard love demons in cadenced argument: *On the Cause Why Things Exist.* He stopped, lost in wandering mazes, mused; ah! There, *we exist!* God's love does not cease against the rivermouth. Kissings. The flag sinks, in aery purposes. *Do* cease to exist; step up softly to vanish to

Want? We will make gold, remedies, oaths. We will visit the Bowels of the Earth. We will dream of the three meninges. O Pia Mater, womb of nature, accept our hyperdulia! (The Hidden Stone is found by Rectification, a soundless, stealthy work. Dripdrop of vitriol into the Earth-Anus.)

The Parable of the Sun and the Moon

The king arrives unaccompanied and enters the paren-
chyma. No other person then draws thither to my skin,
save the guard, R.M., a humble man. The dew Pia water-
ing it, dissolving layers of trodden gold. He gives it to the
toadstools. Everything comes in. He divests himself of his
skin. It is written: *I am the Lord Saturn.* The epithesis of
sin. Saturn takes it and careens (Hoa). All things are Hoa.
He, when once it has been given Him, illapses into prepared matter. O how fall'n! (Squab, upon a rock.) So,
also, is His nose, His doublet of fine velvet, and these
ever-encroaching growths, the nostrils. What is the
(difference)? Jupiter keeps it twenty days.

It is the Moon, who is the third Beloved. Loved life.
(To "live," anagrammatically.) She keeps the nose for
twenty days. The kin are within. "Microprosopus" is a
cause, white as flowers of salt. Thus: Lovingly, the Spirit
descends in a fine white shirt. We consider his gorged
nostrils.

One, but forty days, and sometimes forty, though it
were so that He may be forty. His Sun is yellow.

Then comes a sun most beautiful. Consider (Wisdom):
Heil! A land where goodness does not depend upon
damp luxuriance. Isenheim! It illuminates these environs
more palpably than hearing or distance. A cello! The hairy
shafts of the world banish the night.

Beginning; it is the sun that keeps each strange implication tuned, though the year sings of the year. Never let
the (futhore) slip into the stagnant pools, which have no
being, Annihilators! A part of their portion was the
"milk" within the park (God's park), in being given a
choice between motionlessness and self-knowledge. The
wyverns will be no longer scaly-eyed.

Doleful, doleful he heard.

We proceed thus to the third Article:

"*Objection 1.* It would seem that (God) has never seen
this terrible virescense. We are torn by the counsel of
Augustine saying that (God) for several miles together
would be in the company of such a Ragman that His

107

'poison' could not annihilate anything. Query: What had we best do when He suffocates?

"*Obj. 2.* Further, by His goodness, governing Doubt, one of the wicked ones *is good.* There is no one here (and there is someone) who whisperingly suggests negro songs. Causes of goodness. The pure fool, who says, 'Evil be thou my G-d!' Or in *The Ring.* (Gold!) 'Is *that* what you want?')

"*Obj. 3.* Further, if (God) were to blaspheme, would He so much love these gifts (so freely offered)? Would He demand our latria? The action of corruption has not done it, for He causes one thing to be generated by another. *Non placet!* The body of a 'hog' cannot annihilate anything. Query?

"*I answer that*: Some have held that brush in muddy water. This must be allowed. However it is demonstrated from natural necessity that *He Himself* vomits on me. (Daily) Layers of thin gold scabs are removed, but His nature *cannot change.* Then, what of us? I know osmosis, and that the cell-mud is sweetened with 'symbology raisins.' Cleaving a way inside me for the umbelliferous fetters that (God) has created. Behold, lo!—the pits and pitfalls *please the Lord.* He keeps it forty days and forty nights. I am HE HIMSELF. Eden had they in reason, had He been free to give it to them."

Come, see—the creepers of inner event!

* *

HEAVENLY REFRESHMENTS

Intolerable foreword! That he cannot at once annihilate anything! The just pause before that which tends to non-being. Barb-tailed Scorpio, as Master Dürer demonstrates, cannot *annihilate* anything. Therefore, come, tender little ones—to plash again! Introduce yourselves to my blood's Phlegethon. Ah, how nicely I burn now. Go it, guests! through all my talents!

Now you listen, now you hear the flagellants' invisibly tiny griefs. I would not squander my lamps and oil. Annihilations. It would be so comfortingly like the "dead."

Pale Venus, Pia Mater, accept these few spirochetes.

Weeping, I saw a Satanophany of "Gold"—fascinar-iorum. Osmosis' ore; yet, one suspects somehow the magic of it. (He entreats your discretion.) Ramiform, the column of fluid blasphemies ascended his spine, under-going swift corruption. This neaptide of pus is not easy to extricate.

But how filthy I've become. Lice gnaw me. The Swine God, Love, in giving being to such creatures, removes the scabs of leprosy. Truth: untruth. Can he "annihilate" His grace? No, nor the waters of rivers. But as we have said above, such tissues on a dunghill are enormously con-tradictory to the Catholic faith.

The pilgrims' way led them along a "street." According to Ps. cxxxiv, 6, immortal hatred burns with an even flame. This is the doctrine of A———: see his treatise, *On Annihilation.*

"He ruleth. He does what He will." Here this "noth-ing" is a (most personal) cause. The conatus of all His acts.

That mighty gallery, Anastomosis, primal forest of es-sential being that we call Heart's Blood. Obtunding, he descends on all that tends to non-being; he *descends,* and Frightfulness lurks alongside, who is born of Nothing-ness, and inhabits Here-and-Now. This is the milky spirit to Whom we address these questions. Sphinx winks. His garden is aroused, but she withholds. And again.

It is enormous, of a sort without haecceity. Without prejudice to All-Maker's goodness, it may be called Slug Water. We must venture farther down, beneath God's lily, to the "Fathers." (*Faust, q.v.*) And without preju-dice to his hairy palms, we are farctate with hatred and scorn. We thumb our noses.

Plant life, water rills, quavers, enervations. Greenness re-flects the most flagitious of them (God). His power calci-fies the powdered root. He mends their crooked bills. O Puppet of Ill, annihilate! Annihilate all, and us.

Pieces; nets converging in the sign of Poison; Pisces. Thrice blessed be the (Cause). Violence of swarms of animated corkscrews.

Squiffy with thirst in German lands,
Among the cheering flagellants . . .

Guilds of penitentials marching to a satispaison. As A——— says, *because* God is grown old are these changes come. He draws a universal blank. Goodness? No, he dances. If it pleased him, he would annihilate cause and motion, sequence and event ... the Pentient.

Consider the proliferation of "Cause." You have here this rotting spinal sac that you may come upon knowledge of "God." Then He reaches a dirty, rugate finger into the cerebrum, and

Gra netiglluk ende firseiglie blears. Gra netiglluk ende firseiglie. Netiglluk ende firseiglie blears.

(God.)

1.

The facts, then. Haast threatens that if I do not limit myself to the fact, the whole fact, and nothing but the fact, my dining-room and library privileges will be withdrawn. The library I might forego.

2.

I have refused, however, categorically, to keep a journal. Though my days are numbered, I will not abet their number.

3.

I am much sicker. I have shooting pains in my groin and my joints. I lose half my dinners. My mouth and nose bleed. My eyes hurt, and my vision has, just these last few days, become quite bleary. I have to wear glasses. Also, I am growing bald, but I am not sure that that may fairly be blamed upon the Pallidine.

I suppose that I am smarter. However, I do not *feel* much smarter. I feel, alternately, loggy and hysterical, manic and depressive, hot and cold. I feel like hell. But in Dr. Busk's offices (which she no longer occupies) I have turned out some remarkable performances on various psychometric tests.

4.

Dr. Busk is no longer working at Camp Archimedes. She is not, at least, in evidence. She has been out-of-sight, in fact, since the very evening of Mordecai's death. I have asked Haast for an explanation of her disappearance, but he will only explain in tautologies: She is gone because she is gone.

5.

All the prisoners I have heretofore written of are dead. The last to die was Barry Meade, who lingered on for almost a full ten months. His wit never failed him, and he laughed himself to death over a book of the dying words of famous men. It was a short time after his death that I wrote the first of the three journal entries which so distressed Haast and which prompted his latest and most vigorous insistence on *facts*.

6.

"What is a fact?" I asked him.

"A fact is what happens. The way you used to write— about the people here, and about what you think about them."

"I *don't* think about them, though. Not these people. Not if I can help it."

"Damn it, Sacchetti, you *know* what I want! Write something I can understand. Not this . . . this . . . it's positively antireligious, this stuff of yours. I'm not a religious man, but this . . . you go too far. It's antireligious, and I can't understand a word of it. You start writing a sensible, intelligent journal again, or I'll wash my hands of you. I'll wash my hands, you understand?"

"Skilliman wants me sent away?"

"He wants *you done* away. As a disruptive influence. You can't deny that you're a disruptive influence."

"What use is my journal to you? Why *do* you keep me on here? Skilliman doesn't want me. His little children don't want to be disrupted by me. All I ask is a jug of wine, a loaf of bread, and a book."

I should never have said that, for it was that that gave Haast the lever he needed to move me. For all my cerebration, I am still the same rat in the same box pressing the same bar.

7.

Haast has changed. Since the night of the great fiasco he has grown milder. That glistering boyishness so characteristic of older American executives has left his face, leaving behind a sea wrack of stoicism. His step is heavier. He is careless about his clothes. He spends long hours at his desk staring into space. What does he see? No doubt, the certainty of his own death, which he never believed in till now.

8.

For this last *fact* I am indebted to the guards. They regard me as an upperclassman these days. They make confidences. Assiduous is not happy about the work that duty requires of him. He suspects it may not be altogether right. Like Hans in my play, Assiduous is a good Catholic.

9.

Auschwitz has been published. Since its completion, I have alternately thought it worthless, even evil, and as excellent as it seemed in the very heat of composition. It was in such a humor that I asked Haast's permission to send it to Youngerman at *Dial-Tone*. He killed half the issue as it was going to bed in order to print it. A very kind letter from him telling me news of Andrea and others. They had been having the worst imaginations of me, because Springfield has been returning all mail addressed to me with CANCELED stamped on it. On the phone they were told simply that: "Mr. Sacchetti is no longer with us."

Some few other shorter things published too, though none of my recentest ravings, since N.S.A.'s code-breaking computers return consistent UNCERTAINTY judgments on these efforts. Haast is not alone.

10.

St. Denis is the patron saint of syphilitics—and of Paris. It's a fact.

11.

What *is* a fact? I ask sincerely. If (10) is a fact, it is because everyone agrees that St. Denis is the patron saint of syphilitics—a fact by consensus. Apples fall to the ground, which may be demonstrated, more often than not, be experiment—a fact by demonstration. But I expect it is not facts of either sort that Haas would have of me. If something is a fact by consensus, it is of small account whether or not *I* relate it, whereas facts that are both demonstrable and *news* are of such rareness that the discovery of a single one is enough to justify the efforts of a lifetime spent in the search. (Not, however, my lifetime.)

Well then, what have we left? Poetry—the facts of the interior—*my* facts. And it has been just such facts that I have been offering. In good faith. In dead earnest.

What *will* you have then? Lies? A half poetry of half truths?

12.

A note comes from Haast: "Just simple answers to simple questions. H.H." Then do, please, ask questions.

13.

A note from Haast. He bids me tell more about Skilliman. As H.H. no doubt knows, there is no subject I would rather avoid.

The facts, then. He is a man in his early fifties, of unprepossessing parts and considerable native intelligence. He is a nuclear physicist of the sort that liberals like myself would like to suppose essentially German. The type, alas, is international. Some five years back Skilliman enjoyed a position of some eminence in the A.E.C. His most notable work for that organization was the development of a theory propounding the undetectability of nuclear testing undertaken in ice caverns of a particular construction. This was during the nuclear "moratorium" of that period. The tests were made—and detected by Russia, China, France, Israel, and (ignominy) Argentina. Skilliman's ice caverns were found to have, in fact, a magnifying rather than a masking effect. It was this error that precipitated the recent and most disastrous series of tests and left Skilliman out of a job.

He found work again very quickly—in the same corporation in which Haast is the director of R & D.

113

Despite a security as tight as the Vatican's, rumors had begun to circulate there, in the upper echelons, concerning the nature of the operations at Camp Archimedes. Skilliman insisted upon an exacter account, was refused, insisted, etc. At last it was arranged that he should be made privy to our little atrocity, but only by agreeing to take up residence here himself. When he arrived, Meade and myself were the only survivors of the Pallidine. Once he understood the nature of the drug and had convinced himself of its effectualness, he insisted on being injected with it himself.

14.

A curious fact from history, which seems relevant at this point.

A scientist of the nineteenth century, Aurias-Turenne, developed a theory that chancroid and syphilis were one and the same disease and that by a technique of "syphilization" one might achieve protection, a shorter period of treatment, and security from reinfection or relapse. It was discovered at Aurias-Turenne's death in 1878 that his corpse was covered with scars where he had used his own "syphilization" techniques on himself —i.e., introduced syphilitic pus into open sores on his own body.

15.

Thus, by Skilliman's agency, the experiment has entered a second phase. It begins to accomplish, in fact, what was at first expected of it—those various researches into the Apocalypse that we call "pure research."

He is assisted by twelve "quats" (as he calls them, with a contempt so superb that even they, his victims, must admire it)—former students or assistants, who have, quite willingly, volunteered for the Pallidine. So emulous are we all to know the highest flights of genius—we who stop just this side of Jordan. I am glad I was delivered from the temptation. Would I, I wonder, have succumbed?

On a mountaintop overlooking the endless reaches of the realms of gold—I can hear the tempter's voice even now: "All this can be yours."

Poetry. Full stop.

114

16.

Another fact then, a fact of the rarest vintage.

In an effort to discover whether there was but a single venereal ailment (gonorrhea was then confuscd with the syph), Benjamin Bell, a researcher of Edinburgh, in 1793 inoculated his students with the disease.

A more cautious, but not a nicer, man than Aurias-Turenne.

17.

A note from H.H.: "What in hell is *relevant* about Aurias-Tureen [sic]?" He also inquires the significance of stopping on this side of the Jordan River.

The relevance of Aurias-Turenne—and of my anecdote about Dr. Bell, by extension—is that he seems to be motivated by the same Faustian urge to secure knowledge at any price that is surely the motivation also of our Dr. Skilliman in Camp Archimedes. Faust was willing to renounce all claim to heaven; our Dr. Skilliman, with little expectation of heaven, is ready to forfeit an even more vital good—his life on earth. All this only in order to understand a pathological condition: in A-T's case, syphilis; in Skilliman's case, genius.

For the significance of the Jordan River, may I refer you to Deuteronomy (Chapter 34) and Joshua (Chapter 1).

18.

On Skilliman's character.

He is envious of fame. He cannot speak of certain figures he has known in public life without making it transparently clear that he resents their achievements and capabilities. Nobel Prize winners infuriate him. He can scarcely bear to read a learned monograph in his own field for the thought that it was someone else who conceived it. The more his admiration is compelled by that which is worthy, the more he (inwardly) gnashes his teeth. Now, as the drug begins to have its effect upon him (it has been six weeks now, more or less), one can sense his mounting elation. His joy is that of a mountain climber who passes the markers left by former climbers at their farthest points of ascent. One can almost

imagine him ticking off the names: "There's Van Allen!"
Or, "Now I've passed Heisenberg."

19.

Skilliman's charisma.

This is willy-nilly the age of teamwork. In another
generation, Skilliman insists, cybernation will have advanced far enough that the solitary genius will come
back into fashion—provided he can get a grant large
enough to supply him with the battalions of self-program-
ing computers he will need.

Skilliman dislikes other people, but because they are
necessary to him, he has learned to use them—just as
once, reluctantly, I taught myself to drive a car.
Somehow I get the feeling that he has learned his "in-
terpersonal techniques" from a psychology text, that
when he begins hysterically to scold one of his subordinates
he says to himself: "Now, for a little negative rein-
forcement." Similarly, when he offers praise, he thinks of
carrots. The best carrot at his disposal is simply the opportunity of conversing with him. For the sheer spectacle
of devastation he is unapproachable.

But his chief strength lies in an unerring clear-sighted-
ness for others' weaknesses. He manages his twelve pup-
pets so well because he has carefully selected men who
wish to be maneuvered. As every dictator knows, there is
never a scarcity of such men.

20.

I seem to have had a larger personal impact on H.H.
than I would have thought possible. His latest interoffice
memo reads like a rejection slip from a quarterly: "Your
picture of Skilliman is not *concrete* enough. What does he
look like? How does he speak? What kind of *person* is
he?"

If I didn't know better, I might suspect that he's been
taking Pallidine.

21.

What does he look like?

A man intended by nature to be slim, he is fat in his

116

own despite. But for a scarcity of limbs, he might aptly be represented as a spider—the swollen belly and minimal limbs. Balding, he cultivates the ineffectual vanity of combing long strands of sparse sidehair across his glistening skull. Thick glasses magnifying speckled blue eyes. Rudimentary ear lobes, at which I frequently find myself staring, partly because I know this annoys him. A general insubstantialness, as though his flesh were only so much butter and might be sliced away without doing any harm to the metallic Skilliman within. A very bad body odor (that same butter, gone rancid). A bad smoker's cough. A single perpetual pimple on the underside of his chin, which he calls a "mole."

22.
How does he speak?
With a slight, residual twang: Texas modified by California. The twang thickens when he speaks with me. I think that for him I represent the great Eastern Establishment—that malign cabal of liberalism which long ago rejected his scholarship applications to Harvard and Swarthmore.

But you meant, really—*What does he say?*—didn't you?
I would categorize his conversations so:
A. Remarks expressive of interest in his own or others' researches. (Example: "We must rid ourselves of the old pointillist notions of bombing—of individual, discrete 'bombs.' Rather we must strive now for a more generalized notion of *bombiness*, a sort of aura. I envision it as something like the sunrise.")
B. Remarks expressing contempt of beauty, accompanied by a fairly candid admission of a desire to destroy it wherever found. (The best example of this is the quotation from the Nazi youth leader Hans Yost, which he has had burned onto a pine plaque and hung above his desk: "Whenever I hear the word culture, I release the safety catch of my Browning.")
C. Remarks expressing contempt of his colleagues and acquaintances. (I have earlier quoted Skilliman's opinion of Haast. Behind the backs of even his loyalest quats he scathes—and to their faces, if they step out of line. Once,

when Schipansky, a young programer, said in extenuation of a failure, "I tried, I really did try," Skilliman replied, "But it just wouldn't come up, eh?" An innocent enough jest, except that in Schipansky's case it is probably all too accurate. Indeed, if Skilliman has a tragic flaw it is that, like de Sade, he cannot resist the impulse to wound.)

D. Remarks expressing self-contempt and a hatred of. the flesh, his own or someone else's indifferently. (Example: A joke he made about the Pallidine's effect on "the Rube Goldberg mechanism of the soma." A better example: His preference for the scatological metaphor. He once kept the dining hall in stitches by pretending to have confused eating and shitting.)

E. Remarks and notions that are the fruit of a wild and wide-ranging intellect. Do what I can to construe, I can't turn *everything* he says against him. (In all fairness, a final example. He was trying to analyze the peculiar fascination of lakes, reservoirs, and suchlike large, standing bodies of water. He observed that it is only in these that nature presents us with the spectacle of the Euclidean plane stretching on without apparent limit. It represents that final submission to the law of gravity that is always at work on our cell tissues. From this he went on to observe that the great achievement of architecture is simply to take the notion of the Euclidean plane and stand it on its edge. A wall is such an impressive phenomenon because it is a body of water . . . stood on its side.)

23.

What kind of person is he?

Here, I fear, you would have me leave the realm of fact altogether. Indeed, the preponderance of what I've written about Skilliman is not so much fact as evaluation —and not a very impartial one at that. I dislike the man as I've disliked few people in my life. I think I could say I hate him, if it were not both un-Christian and impolite.

I shall say then that he is a bad person and leave it at that.

24.
Haast replies: "I don't buy that."

What would you have then, H.H.? I have already
wasted more words simply *describing* that son of a bitch
than I've expended on anyone else in this journal. If you
want me to dramatize our encounters, you will have to
ask Skilliman to allow me to spend a little more time
at his side. He dislikes me as much as I dislike him. Except when we both take dinner in the dining room
(where, alas, the quality of the meals has fallen off
sadly), we rarely meet, much less talk to each other.

Would you like me to write fictions about Skilliman?
Have you so far abandoned your faith in facts as to ask
that? Is it a story you want?

25.
A note from H.H. "That will do." He is shameless.
Very well then—a story:

SKILLIMAN,
or
The Population Explosion
A tale by
Louis Sacchetti

Despite the baby's kicking, he had managed to insert
both his little legs into the proper orifices in the canvas
car chair. He was reminded of some particularly difficult
peg-and-slot problem of the sort that chimpanzees are
always being asked to solve on their intelligence tests.

"Too many of the damned things," Skilliman grum-
bled.

Mina, entering on the right-hand side, helped him secure Baby Bill, their fourth, with shoulder straps. The
straps criss-crossed his bib and buckled beneath the seat,
out of his reach. "Too many what?" she asked in-
curiously.

"Babies," he said. "There are too many goddamned
babies."

"Of course," she said. "But that's in China, isn't it?"

He smiled appreciatively at his gravid wife. From the

119

very first her special attraction for Skilliman had been her unfailing incomprehension of anything he might say to her. It was not just that she was ignorant, though she *was* wonderfully ignorant. Rather, it was her refusal to be aware of him, or of anything, that did not contribute directly to the bovine comforts of the immediate moment. His Io, he called her.

Someday, he hoped, she would be just like her mother in Dachau—from whom everything specifically human—intelligence, charity, beauty, volition—had been drained away, as though someone had pulled out a plug from somewhere: the undead Frau Kirschmayer.

"Close the door," he said. She closed the door.

The red Mercury pulled out of its garage, and a little radio device of Skilliman's own designing triggered the mechanism that closed the garage door. Mina, he called his little invention.

When they were out on the thruway her hand reached automatically for the radio knob.

His hand caught hold of her thick-boned wrist. "I don't want the radio on," he said.

The hand, heavy with the ostentation of the zircon ring, drew back. "I was just going to turn on the radio," she explained mildly.

"You're a robot," he said, and leaned across the front seat to kiss her soft cheek. She smiled. After four years in America, her English was still so rudimentary that she didn't understand words like "robot."

"I have a theory," he said. "My theory is that these shortages aren't due entirely to the war, as the government would like us to think. Though, of course, the war does aggravate matters."

"Aggravate . . . ?" she echoed dreamily. She stared at the white lines being sucked into the hood of the car—faster and faster until you couldn't see the separate dashes at all—just a single line of not quite so intense a whiteness.

He turned on the autopilot, and the car began accelerating again. It edged into the densely packed third lane.

"No, the shortages are simply the inevitable result of the population explosion."

"Don't be gloomy again, Jimmy."

"People used to think, you know, that it would level off, that the curve would be S-shaped."

"People," Mina said dismally: "What people?"

"Riesman, for instance," he said. "But those people were wrong. The curve just goes on rising, rising. Exponentially."

"Oh," she said. She had begun to have a vague feeling that he was criticizing her.

"Four hundred twenty million," he said. "Four hundred seventy million. Six hundred ninety million. One point oh nine billion. Two and a half billion. Five billion. And any day now, ten billion. It shoots up off the graph like a Ranger rocket."

Office work, she thought. *I wish he wouldn't bring his office work home with him.*

"It's a fucking hyperbola!"

"Jimmy, please."

"I'm sorry."

"It's Baby Bill. I don't think he should hear his own father talking like that. Anyhow, darling, you shouldn't worry so much. I heard on television that the water shortage will be over by next spring."

"And the fish shortage? And the steel shortage?"

"It's not *our* problem, is it?"

"You always know just what to say to make me feel better," he said. He leaned across Baby Bill and kissed her once again. Baby Bill began to cry.

"Can't you make him shut up?" he asked after a while.

Mina made cooing noises at her only son (the three before had been girls: Mina, Tina, and Despina) and tried to pet his flailing, flanneled arms. At last, discouraged, she forced him to swallow a yellow (for infants up to two years old) tranquilizer.

"It's simply Malthus," he resumed. "You and I are increasing at a geometrical rate, while our resources are only increasing arithmetically. Technology does what it can, but the human animal can do more."

"Are you still talking about those babies in China?" she asked.

"Then you *were* listening," he said, surprised.

121

"You know, all they need there is birth control, like we've got. They have to learn to use pills. And queers— they're going to let queers be legal! I heard that on the news. Can you imagine that?"

"Twenty years ago it would have been a good idea," he said. "But now, according to the big computer at M.I.T., *nothing* is going to level out that curve. It'll hit twenty billion by 2003, come hell or high water. And that's where my theory comes in."

Mina sighed. "Tell me your theory."

"Well, there are two requirements that any solution has to fulfill. The solution must be proportional to the problem—to the ten billion people alive now. And it has to take effect everywhere at once. There's no longer any time for test programs, like those ten thousand women sterilized in Austria. That doesn't accomplish a thing."

"One of the girls I went to school with was sterilized —did you know that? Ilsa Strauss. She said it never hurt a bit, and she enjoys . . . you know . . . just as much as ever. The only thing is she doesn't . . . you know . . . bleed any more."

"Don't you want to hear my solution?"

"I thought you'd told me."

"The idea came to me one day in the early sixties when I heard a Civil Defense siren go off."

"What's a Civil Defense siren?" she said.

"Don't tell me you've never heard any *sirens* in Germany!" he said.

"Oh yes," she said. "When I was a girl, all the time. Jimmy, I thought you said we were going to stop at Mohammed's first?"

"You really want a sundae that badly?"

"The food in that hospital is so terrible. It's my last chance."

"Oh, all right," he said. He returned the car to the slow lanes, took it on manual, and drove off down the Passaic Boulevard exit. Mohammed's Quality Ice Creams was tucked away on a little side street at the top of a short, steep hill. Skilliman could remember the shop from his own childhood. It was one of the few things from thirty years ago that hadn't changed, though sometimes, because of the shortages, the quality of the ice cream slipped.

"Should we take the baby in?" she said.

"He's happy here," Skilliman said.

"We won't be that long," she said. She groaned getting out of the car and put one hand to her swollen belly. "He's moving again," she whispered.

"It won't be long now," he said. "Close that door, Mina."

Mina closed the right-hand door. He looked at the hand brake and at Baby Bill, who was staring placidly at the mock steering wheel of orange plastic that decorated his car chair.

"So long, sucker," Skilliman whispered to his son.

When they were just coming in through the glass door, the counterman shouted at them: "Your car! Sir, your car!" He waved a dish towel frantically at the rolling Mercury.

"What is it?" Skilliman pretended not to understand.

"Your Mercury," the counterman screamed.

The red Mercury coasted, in neutral, in a gently descending curve, down the little side street and into busy Passaic Boulevard. A Dodge hit the right front end and began climbing over the hood. A Corvair, which had been behind the Dodge, swerved to the left and hit the back end of the Mercury, which buckled, accordion-fashion, under the impact.

Skilliman, standing outside the ice-cream parlor, said to his wife, "That's more or less what I was trying to say."

She said, "What?"

He said, "When I was talking about a solution."

The End

26.

And always, inescapably, it comes back to that single fact, the fact of death. Oh . . . that time were not so *liquid* an element! Then the mind might grab hold and wrestle it to a standstill. The angel would have to reveal himself in his eternal aspect then!

But then, in the midst of such Faustian moments, the pain will take hold, and my only wish is that time would accelerate. And so it goes, with rushings to and fro, up and down, from the hot to the cold, and then the rebound.

How many days or hours I've passed since I dashed off my little fable for Haast I have no notion. I am still in the infirmary, as I scribble this, still very sick.

27.

The worst moment came just after I'd written *Skilliman*. I had a mild fit, in the course of which I developed what must have been a hysterical blindness.

I always used to suppose that if I were to become blind I would have to commit suicide. What, if not light, is the mind to feed on? Music is, at best, only a kind of esthetic soup. I am no Milton or Joyce. As Youngerman once wrote:

> The eye is mightier than the ear;
> The eye can see, the silly ear
> Can only hear.

To which, wishfully, I would add:

> If one were blind, one might find
> Some use for ears:
> The human mind
> Can do peculiar things, my dears.

I am too sick to think, to do anything. I seem to feel each thought's pressure against the sutures of my aching brain. Perhaps trepanation is the answer!

28.

There is a really imposing litter of notes from Haast on the bedside table. Excuse me, H.H., if I don't look at them just yet.

I pass the time staring at a tumbler of water, at the grain of the linen of my bedclothes, wishing for sunlight.

Ah, the sensuality of convalescence!

29.

Haast had many complaints to bring against "Skilliman, or The Population Explosion." Chiefly, that it is libelous. H.H. has the true publisher's mentality. That my fiction hinges to some truths (Skilliman *did* marry a German schoolgirl called Mina; her mother *does* live in Dachau; they *do* have five children) only aggravates my fault in Haast's eyes.

("Aggravates . . .?" Haast echoes dreamily.)

Remember, my dear jailer, that you asked for that story, that my only intention was to amplify my thesis that Skilliman is a bad person. The worst, indeed, I've ever known. He quests the grail of Armageddon. As loveless as he is, he would sink to the very lowest circles of Dante's hell—beneath Phlegethon, below the wood of suicides, beyond the ring of sorcerers, to the very heart of Antenora.

30.

A visit from Haast. He is troubled in some way I don't understand. Often he will break off in the middle of a platitude to stare into the sudden silence as though by its agency everything had metamorphosed in that instant to crystal.

What has come over him? Guilt? No, such notions are still beyond H.H. More likely gastric upset.

(I remember something Eichmann is supposed to have said: "All my life I felt fear, but I did not know of what.")

I did ask him, jokingly, if he too had volunteered for the Pallidine. Though he tried to make of his denial another joke, I could see that the suggestion offended him. A little later he asked: "Why? Do I seem smarter than I used to?"

"A bit," I admitted. "Wouldn't you like to be smarter?"

"No," he said. "Definitely not."

31.

H.H. explained at last the reason that Aimée Busk is no longer associated with Camp A. It was not that he had fired her, but that she has run off!

125

"I don't understand," he lamented, "why she would *do* such a thing! When she heard she'd been selected to work on the experiment, she was delighted. Her salary was double here what it had been, and her living expenses were all provided for besides!"

I tried to suggest that a prison can be just as claustrophobic for the guards as for the prisoners, that the same bars enclose both. Haast would not be persuaded.

"She could take a trip into Denver whenever she wanted to. But she never wanted that. She *loved* her work. That's why it makes no sense."

"She must not have loved it as much as you supposed."

Haast moaned. "The security! All the work we've gone to to make this place airtight, and now *this!* God knows what she intends to do with the information she has in her head. She'll sell it to China! Do you realize what those bastards would do with a thing like Pallidine? They're unscrupulous, you know. They'll stop at nothing."

"You've tried to find her, of course?"

"We've tried everything. The FBI. The CIA. All state police have her description. And private detective agencies in all major cities have been put on her scent."

"You could put her pictures in the newspapers and on television."

Haast's laughter verged on hysteria.

"Not a trace of her since she disappeared?"

"Nothing! For three and a half months—not a word. I can't sleep any more for the worry it causes me. Do you realize that that woman has it in her power to wreck this entire project?"

"Well, if she's refrained from exercising that power for three and a half months, there's a fair chance, it would seem, that she'll continue to do so indefinitely. A thought that must have been of great comfort, at one time, to Damocles."

"Who?"

"A Greek."

He left me with a reproachful glance for hurling Greeks at him. What use, in such a world of cares, are Greeks?

How vulnerable these people are who rule the world of cares! I remember the puppy-dog face of the elderly

126

Eisenhower, the fragility of the Johnson persona, such an ill-made thing to begin with.

What an odd mood I'm in today. If I don't stop I'll be compassionating King Charles next! And why not?

32.

The walls are positively *flickering!*

And my breath is short.

At such times I can't tell if it is my genius or my illness that has taken possession.

Ineluctable modality of the *in*-visible!

33.

I'm better now. Or should I say *lower?*

I have been meaning for several days now to create a little Museum of Facts in the manner of Ripley. During my latest stint in the infirmary I developed a sudden craving for newspapers. I have accumulated one entire scrapbook, from which I transcribe these few random excerpts:

34.

Believe It or Not:

The Reverend Augustus Jacks, formerly of Watts, continues to enjoy his extraordinary popular success in the Los Angeles area. National television networks still refuse Jacks permission to broadcast the "Address to a White Conscience" that catapulted the former evangelical minister to overnight fame, on grounds that it is "inflammatory." Their refusal has not prevented most of the nation from having already had an opportunity to hear the address, either on the radio or over local, unaffiliated television stations. The sophomore from the University of Maryland who tried last week to set fire to Jacks' $90,000 Beverly Hills home has consented to accept Jacks' offer of legal aid, after receiving a visit from the Negro minister in his cell in the Los Angeles county prison.

35.

It's a Fact:

The Trip-Trap, another important Las Vegas gambling house, has announced its decision to discontinue blackjack and poker, thus confirming rumors of unprecedented runs of luck against the house at these tables. "Whatever system is being used," William Butler, owner of The Trip-Trap, stated, "it is one that our dealers have never come up against before. Every winner seems to be playing a different system."

36.
Strange as It Seems:

Adrienne Leverkühn, the East German composer of "hard" music, returned to Aspen, Colorado, to appear in court to answer charges brought against her by an association of claimants who maintain that the premiere performance of her *Spacial Fugues* on August 30 this year was the direct and culpable cause of injuries, both physical and mental, done to the claimants. One claimant, Richard Sard, festival director, has testified that the performance ruptured his eardrums, causing him permanent deafness.

37.
Against the Odds:

Will Saunders, a vice-president of Northwest Electronics and rumored to be in line for the presidency, resigned from that company immediately after its recent stock split. He announced his intention to set up his own firm, the precise nature of which he will not divulge. He does not deny the speculations printed in *The Wall Street Journal* to the effect that he controls a patent that could become the basis of a new process of cinematic holography.

38.
This Curious World:

The murderer, or murderers, of Alma and Clea Vaizey is still being sought. Minneapolis police have not yet released to the press all the circumstances surrounding this bizarre and revolting crime, and it is feared that the murderer's boast, made in his "open letter" to the nation's newspapers, may prove all too true—that the murders will seem to have been impossible to perform in the manner in which they were accomplished. Various writers of detective fiction have offered their services to the police.

39.
Stranger Than Fiction:
With three fashion magazines featuring Jerry Breen's *Traje de luces*—or Suit of Lights—in models for both men and women on the covers of their trend-setting fall issues, the success of this fashion innovation is virtually guaranteed. The Suit of Lights is nothing but a transparent web of miniature phosphor-light elements that twinkle in ever-changing patterns of greater or lesser brightness, as determined by the movements and mood of the wearer. Certain gestures of an intimate nature can be programed to produce a momentary "blackout," during which the wearer must depend entirely on his or her own resources. Mr. Breen, in an interview to be printed in *Vogue,* declares his resolution not to move from his present home in Cheyenne, Wyoming, where he has been for many years a designer of western clothes for I. W. Lyle, manufacturers of the *Traje de luces.*

40.
Improbable but True:
S.M.U. continued its tables-turning winning streak by trouncing Georgia 79 to 14. Quarterback Anthony Strether was borne in triumph from the stadium and through the city by a jubilant crowd. In this, the fourth game of the season, analysts detected seven new variations on Strether's complex new "backlash" formation, bringing the total of variant "backlash" plays in S.M.U's repertoire to thirty-one. In the last quarter Coach Olding sent his freshman team onto the field to rub salt into Georgia's already grievous wounds.

41.
Would You Believe It:
A stonemason has been fired from his job at the insistence of the regents of Tulane University. He had

129

carved this epigraph in marble above the entrance of the new library:

THE PEN IS MIGHTIER THAN THE SWORD

The Regents maintain that the stonemason deliberately reduced the space between the second and third words.

42.

I am being tested. Camp A has at last found a replacement for the runaway Busk—Robert ("Bobby") Fredgren, an industrial psychologist in the blithe, California style. Like a basket of August berries, Bobby seems to be compacted of pure sunshine. Tanned, gleaming, and immaculately young, he is what Haast imagines himself to be in his dreams. It will be a pleasure to watch that suntan fading in our Stygian halls.

But it is not his beauty alone I abhor. Rather (much more) it is his manner, mediate between that of a disc jockey and a dentist. Like a d-j he is all smiles and bland chatter, platter after platter of dithering antianxiety songs, of blue skies and sunshine cakes; like a dentist he will insist, even as you scream, that it doesn't really hurt. His dishonesty can withstand the most vigorous assaults; it is well-nigh heroic. This exchange, for instance, from yesterday:

Bobby: Now, when I say begin, turn over the page and begin working the problems. Begin.

Me: My head hurts.

Bobby: Louie, you're not cooperating. Now I *know* you can do splendidly on this test if you'll just put your mind to it.

Me: But my mind *hurts!* I'm sick, you bastard. I don't have to take your goddamned tests when I'm this sick. That's the *rule.*

Bobby: Remember what I said yesterday, Louie—about depressing thoughts?

Me: You said I'm only as sick as I think I am.

Bobby: Hey, that's more like it! Now, when I say begin, turn over the page and begin working the problems. Okay? (With a big bland Pepsodent smile.) Begin.

Me: Fuck you.

Bobby: (Not taking his eyes off his stopwatch.) Let's try that again, shall we? Begin.

43.

Bobby lives in Santa Monica and has two children, a boy and a girl. He is active in local affairs and holds the office of treasurer in his county chapter of the Democratic Party. Politically he considers himself "rather liberal than otherwise." He has reservations about the present war; we should, he feels, accept the Russian offer to negotiate an end to our bacteriological attacks, at least in the "so-called neutral countries." But he thinks the conchies "go too far."

He has good teeth.

He is the very prototype of Sonnlich in my play. Sometimes I get the disquieting feeling that I *wrote* this bland monster into existence.

44.

Bobby, model young executive that he is and (therefore) believer in teamwork, has devised tests for his guinea pigs that must be taken in tandem. Today I had my first experience of this intellectual chain gang. I must confess that I enjoyed it in a simple-minded way, while Bobby was quite beside himself with the pleasure of pretending to be the M.C. of a television quiz show. When one of us would answer some particularly abstruse question, he would cheer: "That's tremendous, Louie! You're doing absolutely *tremendous!* Isn't that tremendous, audience?"

Poor Schipansky, with whom I'm manacled for these events, does not enjoy our games at all. "What does he think I am?" he complained to me. "Some kind of performing monkey?"

Schipansky's nickname among the other quats is Cheeta. His features do bear an unfortunate resemblance to a chimpanzee's.

45.

Another round of tests with Schipansky. I realized last night as I was writing (44) that I wanted very much for the quiz show to go on. Why? And why when my mind is so much more alive other times (I am beginning plans for the construction of a real Museum of Facts in George's abandoned theater; I am doing some interesting poems in

German; I am elaborating baroque arguments against Lévi-Strauss), why should I dwell here on the single hour of the day that I waste at compulsory play?

The answer is simple: I'm lonely. Recess is the only time I can talk to the other kids.

46.

Between rounds today I asked Schipansky what sort of work he was doing with Skilliman. He answered with some technological double-talk that he must have supposed would leave me boggled. I returned the serve neatly, and soon Schipansky was bubbling with confidences.

I gather from these that Skilliman has turned his attention to the possibility of a sort of geologic bomb—something on the order of what happened accidentally at the Mohole, but on a much grander scale. He wants to lift new mountain ranges from the earth. The Faustian urge is always toward the giddy heights.

After a few calm moments picking sprigs of such edelweiss, I touched, ever so gently, on the possible moral implications of such researches. Does every grad student have a clear right to be initiated into the mysteries of cataclysm? Schipansky froze into near catatonia.

In an effort to retrieve my error, I tried to involve Bobby in the conversation, reminding him of his feelings, confided earlier, about bacteriological warfare. Wouldn't, I suggested, geological warfare be rather worse, rather more irresponsible? Bobby couldn't say—it wasn't his field of knowledge. In any case we at Camp A. are concerned only with pure research. Morality is concerned with applications of knowledge, not the knowledge itself. And more balm of that sort. But Schipansky didn't show a sign of thawing. I'd touched the wrong button, absolutely.

That was the end of tests for today. When Schipansky was out of the office, Bobby allowed himself to become as vindictive as it is in his warm nature to be. "That was a terrible thing to do," he fretted. "You've got that poor boy completely *depressed*."

"No, I didn't."

"You *did*."

"Oh, cheer up," I said, patting him on the back. "You're always looking on the dark side of things."

"I know," he said gloomily. "I try not to, but sometimes I just can't help it."

47.

Schipansky came over to my laden table at lunch. "If you don't mind . . . ?" Such self-effacement! As though, had I minded, he would have thrown the switch that cancels his too bold existence.

"Not at all, Schipansky. I appreciate company these days. You new people are not nearly so gregarious as the last flock of lambs." Which was more than mere courtesy. Often I'm quite by myself at meals. Today there were three other quats besides Schipansky dining in the hall, but they kept to themselves, mumbling numbers through their ingenuous pizzas.

"You must feel nothing but contempt for me," S. began, dabbling a spoon unhappily in cold spinach soup. "You must think I don't have a mind."

"After those tests we took together? Not very likely."

"Oh, tests! I've always done well on *tests*, that's not what I meant. But at college your kind of person . . . the arts students . . . they think that just because a person is studying a science, that he doesn't have a . . ." He pushed away his mussed soup with the dribbling tip of his spoon.

"A soul?"

He nodded, eyes fixed in the soup. "But it isn't true. We do have feelings, the same as anybody else. Only perhaps we don't display them so openly. It's easy with your background to talk about conscience and . . . things like that. No one is ever going to offer *you* $25,000 a year at graduation."

"As a matter of fact, I know lots of former classmates, would-have-been poets or painters, earning double that in advertising or television. There's a form of prostitution for everybody these days. If nothing else, one can become a union leader."

"Mmm. What's that you're eating?" he asked, pointing at my plate.

"Truite braisée au Pupillin."

He signaled a black-uniformed waiter. "Some of that for me too."

"I wouldn't have imagined it was really the money that seduced you," I said, pouring him some Chablis.

"I don't drink. No, I guess it wasn't really the money."

"What was your major at school, Schipansky? Biophysics, yes? Didn't you at any point like the subject for its own sake?"

He bolted half a glass of the refused wine. "More than anything else, yes! I like it more than anything else in the world. I don't understand sometimes, I honestly don't understand, why *everyone* doesn't feel the same way I do. Sometimes it's so intense that I . . . I can't . . ."

"I do feel the same way, but about poetry. About all the arts, but most particularly poetry."

"And people?"

"People come next."

"Even your wife, if it came to that?"

"Even my self, if it came to *that*. And now you're wondering how I've got the nerve to come down on you about morality, feeling the way I do, the way we do."

"Yes."

"Because I'm talking about just that—feeling. Ethics is concerned with what one actually does. The temptation and the act are two different things."

"Is art a *sin* then? Or science?"

"Any overweening love, less than the love of God Himself, is sinful. Dante's hell is full, above Dis, of those who loved agreeable things just that bit too much."

Schipansky blushed. "If you'll excuse me for saying so, Mr. Sacchetti, I don't believe in God."

"No more do I. But I did for quite a while, and so you must excuse me when He creeps into my metaphors."

Schipansky chuckled. His eyes flickered up from the table to meet mine for an instant, then retreated to the trout that the waiter had just brought. It was enough to let me know that he had been hooked.

What a career I missed in not becoming a Jesuit. Next to an out-and-out seduction, there is no game quite so absorbing as this of convert-making.

Later:

I've had to spend the better part of the day in darkness listening to music. My eyes . . . how I *resent* my inconstant flesh!

48.

Unprompted, he came to my dim room today to tell me the story of his life. He gave the impression of telling it all for the very first time. No one before this, I suspect, has expressed an interest in the matter. And indeed, it is a cheerless tale—too undeviatingly like the monochrome life one would extrapolate for him on no other basis than a glimpse of the ties in his closet.

The child of divorced parents, S.'s youth was full of discontinuities. He seldom attended the same school for two years running. Though unquestionably bright, he had the extraordinary ill luck always to be the *next*-brightest child in his class, always second-best. "I am," he said, "the essential salutatorian." He became obsessively competitive, straining after that which his rivals obtained without effort. For such a person friendship is impossible; it would imply a cease-fire. S. realizes that he sacrificed his youth to false idols; now, his youth wasted, he sacrifices his life to them.

He is twenty-four, but he has that look of perpetual adolescence so common to science swots: a scant, gangling body, a pallid face, acne, hair just too long to be called crew cut, too short to lie flat. Poached-egg eyes that convey melancholy without inspiring sympathy, perhaps because of the McNamara-type glasses. A prissy trick of pursing his lips before he starts to talk. Not surprisingly, he is as resentful of fair appearances as Savonarola. Strength, beauty, health, even symmetry offend him. When other quats watch sports on television, Schipansky leaves the room. Creatures like Fredgren, who are nothing *but* fair appearance, can arouse in S. such passions of contempt and envy that he tends instantly toward catatonia, this being his primary response to any passion.

(I am reminded of my own rancorous description of Fredgren. I begin to wonder if I am limning Schipansky's

135

THOMAS M. DISCH

features or my own. He comes to seem more and more a nightmare image of myself, of that aspect of Louis Sacchetti that Mordecai as long ago as our school days dubbed "Donovan's Brain.")

Are there *no* redeeming features? His wit, perhaps. But no, for though I've often had to laugh at what he says, he is so invariably the butt of his own jokes—sometimes grossly, sometimes by sly inference—that his wit soon becomes as distressing as his silences. There is something unwholesomely narcissistic about such persistent self-denigration. Self-abuse, might one not better call it?

The pathos of such persons in that their chief (and to some, irresistible) attraction is that they are so *wholly* unlikable. It is the lips of such lepers that saints must learn to kiss.

49.
Stop the press! I have discovered a redeeming feature!

He confessed today, as though shamed by the admission: "I like music." He'd managed to narrate his entire life story without finding the fact that all his free time is given over to this enthusiasm worthy of mention. Within the limits of his tastes (Messiaen, Boulez, Stockhausen, *et al.*) S. is knowledgeable and discerning, though (characteristically) his entire experience of their works derives from recordings. He has never been to a live concert or opera! Schipansky is not one of our social animals, not he! Yet when I admitted to being unfamiliar with *Et expecto resurrectionem mortuorum,* he showed a quite missionary zeal in dragging me to the library to listen to it.

And what a wonderful new use for ears this music is! After *Et expecto,* I heard *Couleurs de la Cité Celeste, Chronochromie,* and *Sept Haikais.* Where have I been all my life? (In Beyreuth, that's where.) Messiaen is as crucial for music as Joyce was for literature. Let me say just this: Wow.

(Was it *I* who wrote: "Music is, at best, only a kind of esthetic soup"? Messiaen is an entire Thanksgiving dinner.)

Meanwhile the work of conversion goes on. S. men-

136

tioned that Malraux had commissioned *Et expecto* to commemorate the dead of the two world wars, and such is the integrity of the piece that it is uncomfortable to discuss the music without touching on that which it commemorates. Like most of his contemporaries, S.'s attitude to history is one of peeved impatience. Its vast absurdities have no power as exampla. But it is difficult, especially with the gold of Pallidine in one's veins, to remain such a perfect ostrich as that.

50.
A note from Haast that he wanted to see me. When I arrived at the appointed time, he was engaged. There was nothing of interest in the anteroom but a book by Valery, which I began to browse through. Almost at once I came to the following passage, which was heavily underscored:

Carried away by his ambition to be unique, guided by his ardor for omnipotence, the man of great mind has gone beyond all creations, all works, even his own lofty designs; while at the same time he has abandoned all tenderness for himself and all preference for his own wishes. In an instant he immolates his individuality. . . . To this point its pride has led the mind, and here pride is consumed. . . . [The mind] . . . perceives itself as destitute and bare, reduced to the supreme poverty of being a force without an object. . . . He [the genius] exists without instincts, almost without images; and he no longer has an aim. He resembles nothing.

Beside this passage, someone had scrawled in the margin: "The supreme genius has ceased at last to be human."
When Haast could see me, I asked him if he knew who might have left the book in his anteroom, suspecting Skilliman. He didn't know, but suggested I check with the library. I did. The last person to check out the book had been Mordecai. Belatedly I recognized his handwriting.
Poor Mordecai! What is more horrible—or more human

—than this terror of feeling oneself no longer a part of the species?

The misery . . . the inexpressible misery of what is being done here.

51.

Haast had had no more urgent purpose in asking to see me than to spend a few minutes talking. He, too, it seems, is lonely. Eichmann was probably quite "lonely" in the Office for Jewish Emigration. Listening to his vague chatter, I wondered if Haast would live long enough to stand trial for *his* crimes. I tried to imagine him inside Eichmann's ghastly glass box.

Busk is still at loose. Good for her.

52.

Schipansky relates an indicative anecdote about Skilliman, from a time six years ago when he was taking a summer session course under him at M.I.T., under N.S.A. auspices.

The course was a survey of nuclear technology, and in one lecture Skilliman demonstrated the process known in the trade as "tickling the dragon's tail." That is, he edged two blocks of radioactive materials together, which at a certain point, never attained, would reach critical mass. S. recounted Skilliman's evident enjoyment of this razorish business. At one point in the demonstration Skilliman, as though by accident, allowed the two blocks to get too near each other. The Geiger counter became hysterical, and the class bolted for the doors, but the security guards wouldn't let anyone out. Skilliman announced that they had all received a fatal dose of radiation. Two of the students broke down on the spot. It was all a joke: The blocks had not been radioactive, and the Geiger counter had been rigged.

This delicious jest had been arranged with the cooperation of the N.S.A. psychologists, who wanted to test the students' reactions in authentic "panic situations." This supports my thesis that psychology has become the Inquisition of our age.

It was as a consequence of that joke that Schipansky began working under Skilliman. He passed the N.S.A.

test by showing no signs of panic, distress, fear, anxiety—nothing but benign curiosity in the "experiment." Only a corpse could have manifested more rooted dispassion.

53.

An engagement with Swagbelly Spiderman, in which, I fear, I was worsted.

Schipansky, visiting me in my room, had asked (curiosity finally getting the upper hand) why I have been so quixotic as to insist on being jailed as a conchie, when I might easily (age, weight, and marital status considered) have sneaked out of armed service unobtrusively. I have never met a person who did not, given the occasion, get around to this subject. (A minor discomfort of sainthood—that one becomes, all unwillingly, the accuser and bad conscience of whomever one meets.)

Skilliman entered, escorted by Rock-Eye and Assiduous. "I hope I'm intruding?" he inquired pleasantly.

"Not at all," I replied. "Make yourself at home."

Schipansky rose. "I'm sorry. I didn't know you needed—"

"Sit down, Cheeta," Skilliman said peremptorily. "I've not come to spirit you off, but to have a chat with you and your new friend. A symposium. Mr. Haast, our playground director, has suggested that I should myself have more to do with this fellow, that he must be given a chance to exercise his special talents as an observer. I fear that I *have* rather overlooked him, that I have not given Mr. Sacchetti ample credit. For—as you, Cheeta, have made me realize—he is not undangerous."

I shrugged. "Praise from Caesar . . ."

Schipansky still hovered indecisively above his seat. "Well, in any case, you won't be needing me. . . ."

"Strangely enough, I *do*. So, sit down."

Schipansky sat down. The two guards arranged themselves symmetrically on either side of the door. Skilliman took a seat, opposite me, with the contested soul between us.

"As you were saying?"

54.

As I reconstruct the scene, the world immediately about me, the world of typewriter, littered table, palimpsest wall, shrinks and swells rhythmically, now bounded in a nutshell, now infinite. My eyes ache; my sweetbreads and brains grow nauseous as though farctate with bad food yet restrained from vomiting.

A stoic, but not stoic enough not to whine a little, not enough not to want a little sympathy.

Get on with it, Sacchetti, get on with it!

(Skilliman was sick today too. His hands, usually so ineloquent, shook with ague. The "mole" beneath his chin has gone all purple, and when he coughs he looses sulfurous smells, as of farts or spoiled mayonnaise. He takes a perverse pleasure in the symptoms of his decay, as though they are all points in the case he is making against his body's treason.)

55.

His monologue.

"Come, come—moralize for us, Sacchetti. Such reticence isn't like you. Tell us why it's good to be good. Lead us by a paradox to virtue—or to heaven. No? A smile is no answer. I won't buy it. I won't buy smiles, paradoxes, virtue, nor yet heaven. To hell with all of them. But I'll buy hell. At least it's possible to *believe* in hell. Hell is that famous bleeding hole at the center of things. You look askance, but there it is, my friend, all too plainly visibly. Put it another way. Hell is the second law of thermodynamics. It is that frozen, eternal equilibrium that makes calamity of so long life. A universal Misrule, all things wound down and nowhere to go. And Hell is more than that. Hell is something we can *make*. That, finally, is its fascination.

"You think me flippant, Sacchetti. You curl your lip, but you don't reply. You know, don't you, better than to try? Because if you were to be at all honest, you'd find yourself on my side. You put it off, but it stares you in the face—the coming victory of Louie II.

"Oh yes, I read your journals. I browsed through some bits of it only an hour ago. Where else do you think I come by this jingling eloquence? There are parts you ought to let Cheeta read too—so that he might try to improve that lamentable personality of his. Face to face, I doubt you are ever so contemptuous of him. It is the

140

lips of such lepers as you, my lad, that saints like Louis must learn to kiss. Dear me, such very Freudian metaphors!

"But we're *all* human, aren't we? Even God is human, as our theologians have discovered to their chagrin. Tell us about God, Sacchetti, that God in whom you profess no longer to believe. Tell us about *values* and why we should buy some. We're both, Cheeta and I, quite deficient in *values*. I tend to find them, like the canons of architecture, like the laws of economics, so arbitrary. That is my problem concerning values. Arbitrary, or what is worse, self-serving. I mean, *I* like to eat too, but that's no reason to elevate peanut butter into the immortal, everlasting Pantheon, for goodness' sake! You sneer at peanut butter, but I know you, Sacchetti—you'll salivate at the sound of other bells. *Pâté de foie gras, truite braisée, truffles.* You prefer French values, but it's all the same chyme by the time it hits your guts.

"Speak to me, Sacchetti. Show me some abiding values. Is there no luster left about the throne of your vanished God? What of power? Knowledge? Love? Surely *one* of the old trinity is worth speaking up for?

"I will confess that power is a little problematical, a little raw, for us moralists. Like God in His more fatherly aspect, or like a bomb, power tends to be rather ruthless. Power needs to be qualified—and, as it were, hedged —by other values. Such as? Louis, why do you remain silent?

"Knowledge—how about knowledge? Ah, I see you'd rather pass over knowledge too. One gets a little sick of that apple, doesn't one?

"So it all boils down to Love, to that need to be *somebody else*'s peanut butter. How passionately the ego longs to burst its narrow confines and spread itself out in a thin paste over just everyone. You will observe that I'm being very general. It's always wisest, when speaking of Love, to avoid particular instances, for these tend to seem self-serving. There is, for instance, the love one feels toward one's mother—the very paradigm of human love, but one cannot think of it without feeling one's lips puckering at the nipple. Then, there is the love one feels toward one's wife, but neither can this escape the Pavlovian aspersion of 'Reward!' Albeit the reward is no longer peanut butter. There are more diffuse loves than these, but even the most exalted, the most altruistic of them seems to have its roots in our too human nature. Consider Theresa's transports, behind the convent walls, when the heavenly Bridegroom descended on her. Oh, if only Freud had never written, how much happier we all would be! Say something in defense of Love—do, Sacchetti. Before it's too late.

"Values! *Those* are your values! Not one of them that doesn't exist to keep our feet steady on the treadmill of life, to keep the cogs engaged at those daily rounds so dear to them—the alimentary canal, the spinning world of days and nights, the closed circuit from chicken to egg, from egg to chicken, from chicken to egg. *Don't you honestly sometimes want to break out?*"

56.
His monologue, continued.

"It's just as well that God is dead at last. He was such a prig. Some scholars have professed to find it odd that Milton's sympathies were with his fiend and not with God, but there's nothing remarkable in that. Even the Evangelist more often purloins his fires from hell than heaven. He certainly gives it much closer attention. It's simply so much more interesting, not to say relevant. Hell is closer to the facts that we know.

"Let's carry our honesty even a little further. Hell is not merely preferable to heaven—it's the only *clear* notion of an afterlife—of a goal worth striving toward —that human imagination has been able to devise. The Egyptians, the Greeks, the Romans originated our civilization, populated it with their gods, and formed, in their chthonic wisdom, a heaven underfoot. Some heretical Jews inherited that civilization, changed its gods to demons, and called heaven hell. Oh, they tried to pretend there was a *new* heaven somewhere up in the attic, but it was a most unconvincing deceit. Now that we've found the stairs to the attic, now that we can zoom about anywhere we choose in that unpopulated and infinite void, the game is up, absolutely, for *that* heaven. I doubt the Vatican will survive to the end of the century, though one should never underestimate the power of ignorance. Oh, not the Vatican's ignorance, for heaven's sake! *They've* always known which way the deck was stacked.

"Enough of heaven, enough of God! They neither exist. What *we* want to hear of now is hell and devils. Not Power, Knowledge, and Love—but Impotence, Ignorance, and Hate, the three faces of Satan. You're surprised at my candor? You think I betray my hand? Not at all. All values melt inperceptibly into their opposites. Any good Hegelian knows that. War is peace, ignorance is strength, and freedom is slavery. Add to that, that love is hate, as Freud has so exhaustively demonstrated. As for knowledge, it's the scandal of our age that philosophy has been whittled away to a barebones epistemology, and thence to an even barer agnoiology. Have I found a word you don't know, Louis? Agnoiology is the philosophy of ignorance, a philosophy for philosophers.

"As for impotence, why don't I allow you, Cheeta, to speak of that? Ah, look at him blushing. How he hates me, and how helpless he is to express his hatred. Impotent in hatred as in love. Don't fret, Cheeta—it is, at root, our common condition. At last, at the end of all things, each atom is by itself—cold, immobile, isolate, touching no other particle, imparting no momentum, kaput.

"And is that such a terrible fate, really? Come that great day, the universe will be much more orderly, to say the least. All things homogenized, equidistant, calm. It reminds me of death, and I like it.

"Now *there's* a value I forgot to include on my list: Death. *There's* something to help us break out of that weary old quotidian. *There's* an afterlife that's not hard to believe in.

"That's the value that I offer you, Cheeta, and to you too, Sacchetti, if you have the guts to accept it. Death! Not just your own individual and possibly insignificant death, but a death of universal dimensions. Oh, perhaps not the heat-death at the end of time—that would be asking too much—but a death that would advance that cause almost perceptibly.

"An end, Sacchetti, to the whole shitty human race. What do you say, my boy—will you buy that?

"Or is my proposition too sudden? You hadn't con-

143

sidered buying an entire set of encyclopedias, is that it? Well, give it time, let it sink in. I can come back in a week, after you've talked it over with your wife.

"But let me say, in closing, that anyone with so much as a grain of self-knowledge knows that he wishes for nothing so much as to be out of it. To be well out of it. We wish, in Freud's eloquent words, to be dead.

"Or to quote yourself: 'O puppet of Ill, annihilate. Annihilate all, and us.'

"The exciting thing, you know, is that it's altogether possible. It's possible to make weapons of absolutely godlike power. We can blow this little world apart the way we used to explode tomatoes with firecrackers. We only have to make the weapons and give them to our dear governments. They can be counted on to carry the ball from there.

"Say that you'll help us? Say you'll lend us, at least, your *moral* support?

"What—still mute? You're really no fun to talk to, Sacchetti, none at all. I wonder what it was amused you in him, Cheeta. Now, if you're ready. I believe that there *is* some work to do."

57.

They left the room together, followed by the guards, but Skilliman couldn't resist coming back for yet one more Parthian shot. "Don't be downcast, Louis. I was bound to get the better of you. Because, you know, I have the universe on my side."

Schipansky was not there to be made distraught, and I allowed myself a riposte. "That's just what I find so vulgar."

He looked crestfallen, for he had come to rely upon my silence. Suddenly he was not Satan at all, but only a middle-aged, balding, seedy administrator of not quite the first rate.

58.

What a convenience it is, after all, to pity our enemies. It spares us the larger effort of hate.

Effort. . . . It is too much effort even to say "It hurts."

144

59.

I am unrecovered. I reproach myself now for my ineffectualness at the moment of confrontation. Silence, though it has always served God very well, was not, after all, *my* buckler and *my* shield. It hurts.

But what reply might I have made? Skilliman dared say what we all dread may be so, and even Christ, finally, had no better argument for his Tempter than *Go Away!*

Ah, Sacchetti, how you always get back to that. The Imitation of Christ.

60.

I am low, low.

The waters of sickness gather about the levee. There are no more sandbags. I watch, from the rooftop of my house, the empty streets awaiting the floods.

(Save me, O God; for the waters are come in unto my soul. I sink in deep mire, where there is no standing. I am come into deep waters, where the floods overflow me.)

I stare once again, in the infirmary, at a water glass. I'm on pain pills all the time now.

No one visits me.

61.

Lower.

I can't read more than an hour at a time before the print begins to rape my eyes. Haast came by (because of my lonesome complaint?) and I asked him if someone might be assigned to read to me. He said he would think about it.

62.

Milton, thou shouldst be living at this hour. Or better, your three daughters. Poor Assiduous cannot read verse, knows no other languages, and balks at long words. At last I set him to reading Wittgenstein. There is a sort of music in the contrast between his perplexed, reluctant delivery and the sibylline syllables.

My edition comes off Mordecai's shelves and is annotated in his hand. Half the time I don't understand the commentaries.

145

63.

Am I better or worse? I scarcely know by what signs I am to interpret any more. I'm on my feet again, though still doped. Assiduous, under my direction, is at work constructing the Museum of Facts from my designs.

The equipment from the magnum opus was still there in the abandoned theater. Haast had it removed to another room but insisted on a most scrupulous delicacy in the handling of it. Superstitions sway us, even dead.

64.

An Addendum:

The Reverend Augustus Jacks has had to postpone his visit to the White House due to an unspecified but acute illness.

65.

A recent Acquisition:

Lee Harwood, the noted Anglo-American poet, has begun to publish compositions written in a language of his own invention. Linguists who have examined these "neologisms" substantiate Harwood's claim that his language is not, in essence, derived from any other language, oral or written. Harwood is attempting to establish a utopian community on the outskirts of Tucson, Arizona, where his language can be spoken and "a suitable culture developed around it." Already three hundred subscribers from twelve states have committed themselves to the project.

66.

I have sent out invitations. The museum opening is scheduled for eleven o'clock tomorrow morning. The invitations were supererogatory, as Haast had already promised me that everyone will be there.

67.

The museum has opened and closed. There was more than enough evidence, and my purpose was achieved.

The first one to take a sum from all the assembled addends was Skilliman. He broke into a fit of coughing before the photos of the Vaizey murders that the killers had so thoughtfully provided for the newspapers. When he had recovered his breath, he turned on me angrily: "How long have you known about this, Sacchetti?"

"None of it was exactly classified information, Doctor. It all came out of newspapers." Of course I had assured myself, through Schipansky, that Skilliman was not a newspaper reader.

By now the light was dawning for most of the quats. They gathered about us, whispering. Haast, confronted with the handwriting on the wall, was looking about helplessly for an interpreter.

Skilliman visibly moderated his upset, steering for civility. "When is the first of these clippings dated, if I might ask?"

"Adrienne Leverkühn premiered *Spacial Fugues* on August 30. However, her case is one of the more problematical. I allowed it into the exhibit because Aspen is so nearby, and because she is certainly a Lesbian."

"Of course!" he said, giving way again to anger. "What an asshole I've been."

"You, too?" I asked cordially. Which he did not take in a spirit of fun. Had he been on even slightly familiar terms with his own body, I'm sure he would have hit me for that.

"What are you two talking about?" Haast asked, pushing his way through the quats. "What *is* this? Why are you all getting worked up about a bunch of . . . news clippings? That was a terrible murder, I'll admit, but the police are bound to get the murderer soon. Is that it? Have you figured out who he is?"

"You're the murderer, H.H. As I've been trying these many months to explain. George Wagner's murderer, Mordecai's, Meade's, and soon enough—mine."

"Nonsense, Louis!" He turned on Skilliman for moral assistance. "He's gone crazy. They all seem to go crazy toward the end."

"In that case the world will soon have caught up with him," Watson, one of the bolder quats, put in. "Because it looks like a sure thing that the whole damned world —the entire country, anyhow—has been infected by your Pallidine."

"Impossible!" Haast declared with still unflawed assurance. "Absolutely impossible. Our security is . . ." And now it reached even Haast. "Her?"

"Indeed," I said. "Aimée Busk. Yes, beyond a doubt—her."

He laughed nervously. "Not old Siegfried? You're not trying to tell me that someone got *her* cherry? Don't make me laugh!"

"If not her cherry," Skilliman said, "then it would seem that the Siegfried Line has been outflanked and attacked from the rear."

Haast's network of wrinkles tightened into a sieve of bewilderment. Then, with comprehension, came disgust. "But who would have . . . I *mean!*"

I shrugged. "Any one of us might have, I suppose. We all had private sessions in her offices. I can assure you it wasn't me. Most likely, Mordecai. If you'll recall, the hero of his novella was based on the good doctor. Also, there was just a hint in the story that the heroine, Lucrecia, was being buggered, though I'll admit that that particular suspicion only comes with, as it were, hindsight."

"Why that son of a bitch! I *trusted* that black-assed bastard like my own son!"

68.

It was some time before Haast could realize that there was more than a personal betrayal involved. Meanwhile Skilliman skulked off, brood under wing, to ponder consequences. I'm convinced that his first and strongest reaction was to feel cheated: He'd wanted so much to put an end to the world himself.

69.

Haast required me to spell it out. I gave him my notebooks and my various estimations of the rate of progress of the epidemic.

Assuming that Busk's adventures began immediately after she left the camp (June 22), then the first fruits of her sowing would have begun to appear by mid- or late August. My estimates of the rate of progress are based on the new edition of Kinsey and so it probably errs in the direction of conservatism. The fact that promiscuity (and VD) is more common among homosexuals would likewise tend to accelerate the process, especially in its early stages when rapid dissemination is crucial. The facts in my museum did show a preponderance of "breakthroughs" in just those areas where homosexuality is thickest: the arts, sports, fashion, religion, and sex crimes.

Within two more months 20 to 35 percent of the adult population will be on their way to soaring genius. *Unless* the government immediately reveals all the facts in the case. Less specific warnings against venereal disease will have no more effect on promiscuity than thirty years of Army training films have had. Less, because nowadays we've come to place our faith in penicillin rather than in condoms. Penicillin, sad to tell, has no efficacy against Pallidine.

70.

I *think* that Haast understands all this now. Nothing but a full revelation of the danger can have any effect. Already, by my graphs, a moiety of professional prostitutes have been infected. The epidemic will move by a geometric progression.

71.

I return to the infirmary at closer intervals. The mind, meanwhile, goes its own way.

"What was I talking about? Oh yes . . ."

I amuse myself with speculations on who initiated so improbable a romance—and why. Mordecai? And would it have been out of a purely personal spite, a last chance to get his own back at the Great White Bitch of America? Or had he some intuition of how Busk would react, and was his revenge more universal?

And La Busk herself—why would she invite the dirty little spirochete in? Had some part of her (her ass, for instance) been waiting around all these years just for the day when some big black buck would break and enter? Or was she more farseeing? Was Mordecai just the necessary tool, a middleman between the coveted disease and her blood? Surely there was *some* element of the Faustian in her submission. Was it part of her plan even then to escape Camp Archimedes with her Promethean gifts? Did Pandora accept the stranger's box only that

149

she might be able to open it the minute he was gone?

Tune in again next week.

72.

All day yesterday Haast was out of reach. It is morning —he still refuses to talk with me.

There is no indication yet on the television (no stir at the White House, no tremors on Wall Street, no rumors straining toward the truth) that an announcement is being prepared. Doesn't the government realize that the news *can't* be delayed? With 30 percent civilian casualties, an industrial society simply cannot *cohere*.

And that is hardly the greatest danger. Consider the sheer disruptive force of so much undirected intelligence suddenly set loose. *Already* the institutions are beginning to show cracks. I doubt, for instance, that our university system will survive. (Or is that wishful thinking?) Religions are already taking off in all directions (e.g., Jacks). Catholicism should be able to maintain at least its clergy in line, thanks to celibacy.

But elsewhere it is exactly the people essential to stability who are likely to become infected: the communications industries, managerial suburbia, law, government, medicine, the educational establishment.

Oh, it will be a spectacular debacle!

73.

My light is spent; I begin the long waiting.

Assiduous grows surly in his unaccustomed service. I am reluctant to tax his goodwill with new demands.

Braille?

But my hands tremble.

There is still the vision of memory—walks in the Swiss hills (lovelier, really, than the mountains), that day along the shingle hunting shells and agates with Andrea, her smile, the unlikely purple of the veins beneath her eyes, and all the radiant still-lifes heaped on the tabletops of the quotidian world.

74.

Laforgue wrote: *"Ah, que la vie est quotidienne!"*

But that, precisely that, is its beauty.

75.

Memory also has its music (she should, after all, for she was the mother of the muses), both heard and unheard. Unheard are sweeter. I lie in my dark bed and whisper:

> Brightness falls from the air;
> Queens have died young and fair;
> Dust hath closed Helen's eye.
> I am sick, I must die.
> *Lord have mercy on us!*

76.

I have not said it, have I? Not in so many words. Not in a single world: blind.

77.

Typing slowly, with my mind always elsewhere. The keys of my typewriter have been notched to enable me to continue this record. And shall I confess it at last? I have become fond of my journal. As lonely as I am now, it is a comfort to have some continuities.

78.

Haast has not visited me, and the guards and doctors will not say whether anything is being done to avert a full-scale epidemic. Assiduous tells me that the radio and television are now forbidden in the infirmary. Perforce, I must believe him.

79.

I never know if he is watching me. If he is, I will probably not be able to see this entry to its end.

From being a distant sympathizer and a willing listener to my complaints, Assiduous has become my tormentor. Each day he carries his cruelties a little further in a spirit of experiment (a titration). At first I tried to frequent public places, the library, the dining hall, etc., but it has become clear—from insinuations, muffled laughter, a missing fork—that these scenes have acted as encouragements. Today as I was sitting down to my morning cup of tea, Assiduous pulled away my chair. There was

151

loud laughter. I think my back was hurt. I've complained to the doctors, but fear has made automatons of them. They make it their principle now never to talk to me, except to inquire symptoms.

When I ask to see Haast, I'm told he is busy. The guards, seeing that I'm no longer relevant to the experiment, take their cue from Skilliman, who taunts me openly with my helplessness, calls me Sampson, pulls my hair. Knowing that I've not been able to hold my meals, he asks: "What kind of shit do you think you're eating, Sampson? What kind of shit have they put on your plate?"

Assiduous must be out of the room, or not reading what I type. I spent most of the day typing out poems in French to drive him off. I've made these same complaints in other languages, but as there's been no response I must assume that H.H. no longer bothers to have translations made of what I write. Or that he no longer cares what becomes of me.

Strange—that Haast has come to seem almost a friend.

80.

Schipansky visited me today, bringing two other quats—Watson and Quire. Though no word was spoken on the matter, the implication was that my silence has won the debate. (Given enough rope, the devil may always be relied upon to hang himself?)

Yesterday and the day before Schipansky had been told I was too sick to see him. He got past the guards at last only by enlisting Fredgren's help—and by threatening to go on strike. I'd been declared off-limits by Skilliman. Fredgren, to get Schipansky into the ward, had to appeal over Skilliman's head to Haast.

The visit, welcome as it was, served chiefly to remind me of my growing alienation. They sat about my bed, silent or murmuring banalities, quite as if I were their dying parent, to whom nothing can be said, from whom nothing may be expected.

81.

I did not dare, while they were here, ask what date it is. I have lost track. I don't know how much time I may legitimately expect. I don't *want* to know. My wretchedness reaches that pitch that I hope it is sooner rather than late.

82.
Feeling
a little
better.

But not much. Schipansky brought Sarch's new recording of Messiaen's *Chronochromie*. Listening to it, I could feel the cogs of my mind slowly engaging in the gears of reality. Schipansky didn't say five words the whole while.

Blind, there are so few cues by which to interpret silences.

83.
Schipansky is not my only visitor. Assiduous, though I've dispensed with his services, often finds occasion to play his little tricks on me, chiefly at mealtimes. I've learned to recognize his footsteps. Schipansky assures me that Haast has promised to restrain him, but how, after all, is one to be guarded against one's guards?

84.
Often after a pain shot there is an epiphanic moment when the mind seems to pierce the veil of appearance. Later, back in the real world, I look at the nuggets I've brought back from the far reaches and find they are fool's gold. Don't ask whom the joke is on; the joke's on me.

Chagrin—that the mind is, even now, no more than a tub of chemicals, it's moment of truth a function of its oxidation rates.

85.
Thomas Nashe still haunts me. I tell his rhymes like rosary beads.

> Physic himself must fade;
> All things to end are made;
> The plague full swift goes by;

153

THOMAS M. DISCH

I am sick, I must die—
Lord have mercy on us!

86.

Schipansky, Watson, Quire, and a new convert, Berness, spent the day watching over me in rotation. This, in defiance (though they deny it) of Skilliman's explicit orders. Most of the time they pursue their own interests, but sometimes they will read to me, or we talk. Watson asked if, from my new and higher vantage, I would, given the chance anew, still be a conchie. I couldn't decide, and I suppose that means I would. How many things we do only to seem consistent!

87.

Schipansky has at last overcome his terror of confidences. Since the evening that Skilliman interrupted us, Schipansky has been engaged in the same unbalanced dialogue between the eloquent forces of evil and the reticent forces of good.

"I kept telling myself I had to find a *reason*. But reasons always came in pairs—pro and contra, thesis and antithesis, perfectly matched. At last it was a completely irrational consideration that turned the trick. I was listening to Vickers sing the hunting aria from *Die Frau Ohne Schatten*. Just that. And I thought—if only *I* could sing like that! I suppose it's impossible, of course, considering my age and everything. But I really wanted that, in a way I've never wanted anything else. And that must have been what I'd been waiting for, because afterward there just didn't seem to be a dilemma.

"If I ever get out of here, and if I don't have to die, that's what I'm going to do with myself. I'm going to study voice. And knowing that, having made that decision, I feel . . . just great. And now that I want to live, the hell of it is I won't."

"What do you intend to do with the time that's left here?" I asked.

"I've started to study medicine actually. I've already had a fair amount of biology. It isn't hard. So much of what they have to go through in medical school is really beside the point."

154

"And Watson and Quire and Berness?"

"The project was Watson's originally. He has the ability, which I envy him, to believe that what he's doing at any moment is the only logical and moral thing that can be done. Skilliman couldn't get anywhere talking with him, and his pigheadedness is a help for all of us. Also, now that there are four of us—five if we can count you —it's easier not to be upset by what he says, the threats he makes."

"Do you think there's any chance?"

Minutes of silence. Then: "I'm sorry, Mr. Sacchetti. I forget that you can't see me shake my head. No, not really much of a chance. Finding a cure will always be a matter more or less of trial and error. It takes time, money, equipment. Mostly, it takes time."

88.

H.H. tells me that the officers of his nefarious corporation refuse to admit the existence of the epidemic. Several doctors who have discovered the spirochete independently have been paid off or silenced in some less congenial way.

Meanwhile the headlines in the newspapers grow daily more bizarre. Another wave of super-murders has started in Dallas and Fort Worth. There have been *three* museum robberies in a single week, and the City Council of Kansas City has hired Andy Warhol as Commissioner of Parks. Truly, the world is ending. Not by ice and not by fire, but by centrifugal force.

89.

A stroke. My left hand is paralyzed, and I type this with my right forefinger, a laborsome task.

Mostly, I contemplate the immensity of my darkness, or apostrophize, Miltonically, the holy light.

90.

Songs, Nashe's or my own, console me now no more than Muzak. The very highest thoughts, pierced with this dread, plummet to earth, snapping the branches of trees.

The hunter comes upon it, not quite, it is not quite

155

dead. A wing lifts, goes limp, and lifts again. Not quite, not quite dead.

91.

Flesh falls apart. The lungs strain, and the stomach manufactures incorrect acids. Every meal nauseates, and I've lost thirty pounds. I would rather not walk. Heartbeat erratic. It hurts when I talk.

Yet I am *still* afraid of the darkness, of that dark box.

92.

If only I *were* a cocoon! If only one might believe the dear old metaphors! If only, in these last days, I might become a little more stupid!

93.

Skilliman has gone off to fetch guards, while Quire seeks Haast. There has been something like a confrontation, which, briefly, to recount:

Schipansky & his 3 friends came to my bedside, bringing 2 more quats. With these on our side, Sk's assts will be split evenly 6 to 6. Conversation revolved, as ever, around the poss. of a cure. Today we must have reached critical mass, for we at last broke out of the usual rut of purely medc. solutions. Among the doz. & more unpracticeable conceits there may be *one* that will turn in the lock! (Tho it was no doubt by such desperate reasoning that M. fastened on his alchemic project.) We talked of: studies in mech. brain-wave duplication & storage; Yoga, & other methods of susp. animation, such as freeze-drying, until such time as a cure is developed; even, so help me, time travel—&, as an equiv., interstellar voyaging for a sim. purpose, i.e. returning to a world that would be (in an unrelativistic sense) in the future. Sch. even put forward the suggestion that a global effort to wrest some response from God might be made, since we are after all asking for miracles. Bold Berness suggested escape (!!!!) to which I obj. that there is so little opport. for secrecy that our plot would have to be able to work even if the guards knew of it from the start. Time is up. A pity, I did so want to reach 100.

94.

The Lord is my light and my salvation; whom shall I fear? the Lord is the strength of my life; of whom shall I be afraid?

When the wicked, even mine enemies and foes, came upon me to eat up my flesh, they stumbled and fell.

Though an host should encamp against me, my heart shall not fear: though war should rise against me, in this will I be confident.

One thing have I desired of the Lord, that will I seek after; that I may dwell in the house of the Lord all the days of my life, to behold the beauty of the Lord, and to enquire in his temple.

I am so splendidly, so wildly, so simply, so against-all-expectation *happy!* I am overcome by happiness as by some gigantic benevolent steamroller, crushed by goodness. I can see. My body is whole. My life is given back to me, and the world, the lovely home-again world will not go off to Armageddon without at least a chance to refuse its marching orders.

I am obliged, I fear, to explain. But I only want to sing!

Sequence, Sacchetti, sequence! A beginning, a middle, and an end.

Entry 93 (above) was terminated by the re-arrival in the infirmary of Skilliman with a number of guards, among them Assiduous.

"All right, my little pus-faces, it's time to take yourselves away; Mr. Sacchetti is much to sick to be receiving visitors."

"I'm sorry, Doctor, but we're staying here. We have Mr. Haast's permission to do so, you know." This, quaveringly, from Schipansky.

"You will either, the six of you—where is Quire?— walk out that door by your own power and instantly, or you will, one by one, be carried out. And I have asked the guards to exercise such small brutalities as they find, in conscience, they may. Would someone please remove that disagreeable hand from that noisy typewriter?"

It was, expectably, Assiduous who undertook this

task. I tried to turn away from the typewriter with an appearance of calm, but Assiduous must have been quite close by (Were the guards by now dispersed throughout the room?), for he was able to catch hold my right hand and, in pulling me from my chair, to twist it with an exquisite sense of the excruciating. (A little gasp of satisfaction broke from his lips.) The pain did not leave me for minutes, indeed not till the very end.

"Thank you," Skilliman said. "And now, gentlemen, to demonstrate . . ."

This ellipsis was occasioned by the arrival of Haast with Quire. H.H. began in a puzzled voice: "I've just been led to understand—"

"Thank heaven you've arrived, General!" Skilliman burst out, improvising coolly. "A very little longer and you might have had a full-scale mutiny on your hands. The first thing you must do—before I can discuss the present danger with you—is to have these young men sent each to his own chamber."

The six quats interrupted with a clamor of protest and explanations, but above these turbulent waters Skilliman's shrill oratory overarched, a distinct hyperbola of steely orange: "General, I *warn* you—if you do not separate these young conspirators, each from each, the security of Camp Archimedes will be gravely jeopardized. As you value your career and good name, Sir, take my advice!"

Haast gave only an ambiguous mumble, but must have accompanied it with a sign for the guards to obey Skilliman. The quats were taken, protesting, out of the room.

"I think," Haast began, "that you may be magnifying a mountain into a molehill." He stopped, sensing he'd gone wrong somewhere, puzzling it out.

"May I suggest, General, before we discuss these matters any further that we leave Sacchetti to the attentions of the medical staff? There are . . . some things . . . I would not want him to hear."

"No! He has some reason for asking that, Haast. Settle my fate now and before me, or it may be a pointless discussion. I *suspect* him."

"Shit on his suspicions! It's *security* that's at issue. Or if you must let the corpse have its way, then let it accompany us above."

158

"Above, where?" Haast asked.

"*Above*—you've given me permission to ascend there often enough before this. Why do you balk now?"

"Balk? I'm not balking! I just don't understand."

"I don't want to discuss the matter *here!*"

(Even now I am not sure what Skilliman's intention had been in insisting on this point, which was to prove decisive in so unforeseeable a way. For, surely, it *was* unforeseen? Was it simply a conviction that if he could have his way, all arbitrarily, in this, he could have it in any matter?)

"All right," Haast said, his age audible in the (ever more customary) acquiescence of his voice. "Help Sacchetti along, will you?" he asked of the guards. "And find some sort of overcoat for him. Or blankets. It's cold up there."

It was many times over the longest trip I've taken on one of our elevators. The six of us (Assiduous and two other burly guards were required to prevent my escape) made the ascent in a silence perfect but for the popping of my ears.

Outside the elevator cage, Haast said, "And now you really must stop this mystery-making and explain what is the matter. What has Louis done that is so dreadful?"

"He has attempted a mutiny, and he has very nearly brought it to success. But it wasn't here I wished to go. It will be safer . . . outside."

The guards led me, a hand in each oxter, across the uncarpeted floor, through one door, through another, and then I felt a breath on my face, like the breath of a beloved whom one has believed dead. I stumbled down three steps. The guards released their grip.

Air!

And beneath my slippered feet not the Euclidean spareness of concrete but the unaccustomed and various-textured earth. I cannot say just what I did, whether I cried aloud, or if tears fell from my blind eyes, or how long I continued with my face pressed against the cold rock. I was beside myself. I felt such a degree of happiness as I had never felt in my life before: because this was the actual air and undoubted rock of the world from which, so many months before, I'd been removed.

159

They had been talking together perhaps several minutes. I cannot remember now if it was Haast's amazed "What!" that roused me, or the extreme cold, or simply the returning sense of my danger.

"Kill him," Skilliman said levelly. "Now, you *can't* ask me to be clearer than that."

"Kill him?"

"While he's trying to escape. You see, his back is turned on us. He's lost his blankets in his flight. You are obliged to fire. It's a scene absolutely hoary with tradition."

Haast must have indicated some further reluctance, for Skilliman pressed on:

"Kill him. You must. I have shown logically how his continued presence at Camp Archimedes can have but one consequence. His increasing intelligence will soon make it impossible for *any* of us to be quite certain when we're with him just what kind of clever web he's tying round us. I told you what he was talking to them of today—escape! He said it would have to be an escape that could be made despite our overhearing all their plans! Imagine the *contempt* he must feel for us! The hate!"

I could see, in imagination, Haast's head swaying weakly from side to side. "But . . . I can't. . . . I can't. . . ."

"You must! You *must! You must!* If not you yourself, then designate one of the guards. Ask for a volunteer. One of them will be willing to assist you, I'm sure."

Assiduous presented himself at once, with assiduity. "Me, sir?"

"Stand back, you!" Haast said, with no trace of weakness in his voice. Then, in a diminished manner, to Skilliman: "I couldn't allow one of the guards . . . to . . ."

"Then use your *own* gun sir. Unless you do it, and at once, you will never be sure that you're not caught, already, in his web. You've created this Frankenstein monster, and you must destroy it."

"I could not, myself. I've known him . . . too often . . . and . . . but you? Could you? If the gun were in *your* hand?"

"Give it me! I'll answer you direct."

"Guard, give Dr. Skilliman your gun."

In the long silence after this exchange I stood up and turned around, to receive the rawness of the wind in my face.

"Well? Well, Sacchetti? Don't you have something you'd like to say? A couplet to leave as legacy? Another cheek?" There was that in the intensity of his voice which suggested that he was not quite securely mounted in the saddle of his will.

"One thing. To thank you. It's been so beautiful, coming here again. So inexpressibly beautiful. The wind. And . . . can you tell me, please? Is it night . . . or day?"

Silence in reply, then a gunshot. Another. Seven in all. After each my happiness seemed to bound to a new diameter.

Alive! I thought. *I am alive!*

The seventh shot was followed by the longest silence. Then Haast said: "It's night."

"Skilliman . . . ?"

"He fired his bullets at—the stars."

"Literally?"

"Yes. He seemed to be trying especially for Orion's Belt."

"I don't understand."

"You weren't, in the showdown, a big enough target, Louis, for the considerable grandeur of his spite."

"And the last bullet? Did he commit . . . ?"

"Perhaps he wanted to, but didn't quite dare. *I* fired the last shot."

"I don't understand yet."

In a baritone thickened by catarrh, Haast hummed the tune of "I'll Build a Stairway to Paradise."

"Haast," I said. "Are you . . .?"

"Mordecai Washington," he said. He laid two blankets back on my shoulders. I began to consider.

"We'd really do best now to return downstairs."

95.
Elements of a Denouement.

Haast/Mordecai conducted me to the room just off the old theater where, when I was building my Museum of Facts, the equipment from his magnum opus had been stored. The guards were more preoccupied with Assiduous than with me; Ass. made loud, bolking protests at their rough handling.

The equipment was set up as it had been on the evening of the great fiasco (as I had then judged it). Ass. and I took the places, respectively, of Haast and Mordecai. With a numbed, grateful suspension of all ratiocination I allowed myself to be strapped and fitted. I must by then have realized, if whisperingly, what was afoot, and I must hold myself to blame for the consequences. I remember going blank when the switch was thrown. Opening my eyes I saw . . .

And that was half the wonder—*I saw!*

. . . my own body, a sack of diseases and old flesh, very nearly dead. That body stirred; its eyes opened—to darkness; its hands moved up to its face; its face screamed.

I looked down at my own flesh with an almost swooning admiration. *May* I call it my own? Or does it belong, in large part yet, to Assiduous?

96.
Elements of a Denouement, continued.

Mordeaci explained how, in their first months in Camp A., a code had been devised by which the prisoners could communicate secretly without arousing suspicion. All their "alchemic" twaddle had been a crypt, a code of more than Egyptian complexity and complicated by frequent flights of free-form fancy—static, in effect—the better to boggle the N.S.A. computers. Once this language had been established, several researches were undertaken, but the most promising proved one which Schipansky et al. had touched on peripherally at our most recent brainstorming: mechanical brainwave duplication and storage, following the lines of Frawley's work at Cambridge. The consideration that had stopped *us* had been how to get the brain-thing *out* of storage? The only sensible container for it would be another human body.

Mordecai and his fellows drew this conclusion, and the next—that any device they developed must accomplish recording and playback at one go. *I.e., it would be a mind reciprocator.* That they were able to develop such an instrument with a minimum of actual experiment, maintaining all the while the imposture of the "magnum opus," that they could design it in a manner that disguised its intended use from the electronics engineers who had been called in to testify to its innocuity, and that they could bring it to so successful an issue at its first operation—this is the most awesome testimony that I have yet seen to the power of Pallidine.

(One small after-the-fact irony. I had seen the wiring diagram for the main component of the reciprocator hidden in the manner of Poe in the jumble of papers on M.'s desk. It was the drawing I'd found in George Wagner's *Expense Book* of a "king" and the lattice of heads.)

97.
Elements of a Denouement, concluded.

It was a happy accident that Haast's mind, finding itself suddenly in Mordecai's exhausted frame, should panic so hectically as to produce an embolism. Mordecai maintains that it was the thought of being a Negro that undid him.

To think of Haast being dead these many months and my visiting with him all the while! Going back over it, I see that many of the changes I'd observed in Haast might have been read as clues, but on the whole it was an immmensely well-executed imposture.

But to what purpose, this imposture? Mordecai explained the necessity of a gradual takeover, pointing out that he could exercise Haast's authority only as long as he behaved in a plausibly Haast-like way. A prisoner even after he'd become the warden!

Gradually the other prisoners (the Bishop, Sandemann, etc.) used the mind reciprocators to infiltrate the staff of Camp A. taking sometimes a member of the medical staff and sometimes a guard as their "replacement bodies." One of the strangest consequences of my arrival here was that by the example of my nonviolence I persuaded three of the prisoners, Barry Meade among them, to forego "resurrection!" Each chose to die his own death rather than condemn someone else to it.

It was for fear that I would have insisted on a similar self-sacrifice that Mordecai maintained his mystery till the very end, till I had inherited, irreversibly, my victim's flesh. Would I have insisted on martyrdom? I am so in love now with that flesh, with life and health, I cannot believe it. I probably would have!

98.

Meanwhile, the future. The search is already well under weigh for a vaccine. Hope shines bravely from twenty accessible peaks. And if we go down, we'll at least go down fighting.

So, sing heigh-ho!

99.

No, it is not as jolly as all that. There is terror too. Behind the mask of Haast/Mordecai's face lurks the dark knowledge of another, further-off future, of a height beyond the first rosy peaks, of a coldness and strangeness extreme as death. Valery is right! Finally the mind *is* destitute and bare. Finally it is reduced to the supreme poverty of being a force without an object.

I exist without instincts, almost without images; and I no longer have an aim. I resemble nothing. The poison has had not two effects—genius and death—but one. Call it by which name you will.

100.

A good round number to end on.

It is December 31, another tidiness. Today Mordecai said: "Much that is terrible we do not know. Much that is beautiful we shall still discover. Let's sail till we come to the edge."

ABOUT THE AUTHOR

THOMAS MICHAEL DISCH became a freelance writer in 1964 after working in advertising. He was born in Iowa in 1940, and was educated at NYU. His first published science fiction story, "The Doubletimer," appeared in *Fantastic* in 1962. His novels include *The Genocides, Echo Round His Bones, 334;* he has also published several short story collections, most recently, *Getting Into Death.* His new novel, *On Wings of Song,* will be a Bantam paperback in the near future. Disch was involved with the popular television series, *The Prisoner,* and has edited several anthologies of short fiction.

FANTASY AND SCIENCE FICTION FAVORITES

Bantam brings you the recognized classics as well as the current favorites in fantasy and science fantasy. Here you will find the beloved Conan books along with recent titles by the most respected authors in the genre.

☐	01166	URSHURAK	
		Bros. Hildebrandt & Nichols	$8.95
☐	13610	NOVA Samuel R. Delany	$2.25
☐	13534	TRITON Samuel R. Delany	$2.50
☐	13612	DHALGREN Samuel R. Delany	$2.95
☐	11662	SONG OF THE PEARL Ruth Nichols	$1.75
☐	12018	CONAN THE SWORDSMAN #1	
		DeCamp & Carter	$1.95
☐	12706	CONAN THE LIBERATOR #2	
		DeCamp & Carter	$1.95
☐	12970	THE SWORD OF SKELOS #3	
		Andrew Offutt	$1.95
☐	12026	THE ROAD OF KINGS #4	
		Karl E. Wagner	$1.95
☐	12031	SKULLS IN THE STARS: Solomon Kane #1	
		Robert E. Howard	$1.95
☐	11276	THE GOLDEN SWORD Janet Morris	$1.95
☐	13426	DRAGONSINGER Anne McCaffrey	$2.25
☐	13360	DRAGONSONG Anne McCaffrey	$2.25
☐	12019	KULL Robert E. Howard	$1.95
☐	10779	MAN PLUS Frederik Pohl	$1.95
☐	12269	TIME STORM Gordon R. Dickson	$2.25

Buy them at your local bookstore or use this handy coupon for ordering:

OUT OF THIS WORLD!

That's the only way to describe Bantam's great series of science fiction classics. These space-age thrillers are filled with terror, fancy and adventure and written by America's most renowned writers of science fiction. Welcome to outer space and have a good trip!

☐	11392	**STAR TREK: THE NEW VOYAGES 2** by Culbreath & Marshak	$1.95
☐	13179	**THE MARTIAN CHRONICLES** by Ray Bradbury	$2.25
☐	13695	**SOMETHING WICKED THIS WAY COMES** by Ray Bradbury	$2.25
☐	12753	**STAR TREK: THE NEW VOYAGES** by Culbreath & Marshak	$1.95
☐	13260	**ALAS BABYLON** by Pat Frank	$2.25
☐	13006	**A CANTICLE FOR LEIBOWITZ** by Walter Miller, Jr.	$2.25
☐	12673	**HELLSTROM'S HIVE** by Frank Herbert	$1.95
☐	12454	**DEMON SEED** by Dean R. Koontz	$1.95
☐	11662	**SONG OF THE PEARL** by Ruth Nichols	$1.75
☐	13766	**THE FARTHEST SHORE** by Ursula LeGuin	$2.25
☐	13594	**THE TOMBS OF ATUAN** by Ursula LeGuin	$2.25
☐	13767	**A WIZARD OF EARTHSEA** by Ursula LeGuin	$2.25
☐	13563	**20,000 LEAGUES UNDER THE SEA** by Jules Verne	$1.75
☐	11417	**STAR TREK XI** by James Blish	$1.50
☐	12655	**FANTASTIC VOYAGE** by Isaac Asimov	$1.95
☐	12477	**NEBULA AWARD STORIES ELEVEN** Ursula LeGuin, ed.	$1.95

Buy them at your local bookstore or use this handy coupon for ordering:

Bantam Books, Inc., Dept. SF, 414 East Golf Road, Des Plaines, Ill. 60016

Please send me the books I have checked above. I am enclosing $_____ (please add $1.00 to cover postage and handling). Send check or money order —no cash or C.O.D.'s please.

Mr/Mrs/Miss_____

Address_____

City_____State/Zip_____

SF—2/80

Please allow four to six weeks for delivery. This offer expires 8/80.

Bantam Book Catalog

Here's your up-to-the-minute listing of over 1,400 titles by your favorite authors.

This illustrated, large format catalog gives a description of each title. For your convenience, it is divided into categories in fiction and non-fiction—gothics, science fiction, westerns, mysteries, cookbooks, mysticism and occult, biographies, history, family living, health, psychology, art.

So don't delay—take advantage of this special opportunity to increase your reading pleasure.

Just send us your name and address and 50¢ (to help defray postage and handling costs).